Born in Lincolnshire in 1912, **Michael Francis Gilbert** was educated in Sussex before entering the University of London where he gained an LL B with honours in 1937. He joined the Royal Horse Artillery during World War II, and served in Europe and North Africa, where he was captured and imprisoned – an experience recalled in *Death in Captivity*. After the war he worked in a law firm as a solicitor, and in 1952 he became partner. Gilbert was a founding member of the British Crime Writers Association, and in 1988 he was named a Grand Master by the Mystery Writers of America – an achievement many thought long overdue. He won the Life Achievement Anthony Award at the 1990 Boucheron in London, and in 1980 he was knighted as a Commander in the Order of the British Empire. Gilbert made his debut in 1947 with *Close Quarters*, and since then has become recognized as one of our most versatile British mystery writers.

FICTION:

THE DANGER WITHIN
BE SHOT FOR SIXPENCE
AFTER THE FINE WEATHER
THE CRACK IN THE TEACUP
THE DUST AND THE HEAT
THE ETRUSCAN NET
FLASH POINT
THE NIGHT OF THE TWELFTH
THE EMPTY HOUSE
THE KILLING OF KATIE STEELSTOCK
THE BLACK SERAPHIM

INSPECTOR HAZLERIGG SERIES:

CLOSE QUARTERS
THE DOORS OPEN
DEATH HAS DEEP ROOTS
FEAR TO TREAD

PATRICK PETRELLA SERIES:

GAMES WITHOUT RULES
STAY OF EXECUTION
PETRELLA AT Q
MR CALDERS AND MR BEHRENS
THE YOUNG PETRELLA
ANYTHING FOR A QUIET LIFE

MICHAEL
GILBERT
BLOOD AND JUDGEMENT

HOUSE OF
STRATUS

This edition published in 2004 by House of Stratus, an imprint of
Stratus Books Ltd., 21 Beeching Park, Kelly Bray,
Cornwall, PL17 8QS, UK.

www.houseofstratus.com

Typeset, printed and bound by House of Stratus.

A catalogue record for this book is available from the British Library
and the Library of Congress.

ISBN 0-7551-0513-3

Dedicated to the Divisional Detective,
with admiration and respect

Contents

1

"Remember, Remember..."

The room behind his shop, where Mr Robins carried on the pawnbroking section of his Jeweller's, Silversmith's and Pawnbroker's Establishment, was lit by half a dozen powerful electric bulbs. This was policy, for some of the goods that Mr Robins handled repaid the closest scrutiny.

He pushed his glasses up onto his forehead and said, "Yes. It looks very like it."

"I'm afraid it is," agreed Detective Sergeant Petrella, folding up the old pawn list that they had been studying together. "Clasp, white metal filigree with a single white zircon-cut diamond of about two carats set centrally. The filigree's been hammered flat and given a sort of new look, but there's no disguising the stone."

"You'd have to hit a diamond pretty hard to alter *its* shape," agreed Mr Robins. "Well, it looks as if I'm the mug. Who's it belong to?"

"Part of a mixed lot lifted three years ago from Colegraves. One of their smaller North London branches. Not far from here, as a matter of fact."

"And I suppose it's been sitting for three years – under the floor boards in someone's back kitchen, waiting for the heat to go off, and some mug to buy it or lend on it." Mr Robins consulted his great leather-bound, brass-edged ledger. "Forty quid."

"You'll get it back from your insurance company."

"Like getting teeth out of a month-old corpse, I will," said Mr Robins.

"Who did you say the depositor was?"

Mr Robins again consulted his ledger, the repository of so many family secrets that he never let it out of his sight by day and locked it up each evening with his own hands in the old-fashioned safe which was built into the masonry of the backroom chimney.

"King," he said. "Albert King. Occupation, fitter. Address, 45 Upper Green. Date of deposit, October 12."

"I suppose you can't give me a description?"

"Now, really – "

"Perhaps that is a bit unreasonable."

"If you ask my honest opinion," said Mr Robins, "the only bit that's true out of the whole of that little lot's the date. I know that's correct. I wrote it myself."

"I expect you're right," said Petrella. But he put it all down in his book. In police work the first rule was never to neglect the obvious.

"Any idea who pulled this?" asked Robins, closing his ledger.

"We're not certain. But it could have been one of Ritchie's jobs."

" 'Monk' Ritchie?"

"That's right."

"But he's been inside nearly a year."

Petrella made a tiny mental note that it might be worth keeping an eye on a man who knew the nickname of criminals and exactly when they went to prison.

"That's right," he said. He pocketed the clip, now wrapped in tissue paper, and as he turned to go, added, "He went up for five years, last Christmas. Breaking and entering, and violence. It's a pity he didn't qualify for Preventive Detention, then we might have been shot of him for a nice long time."

"But if he's inside – " said Mr Robins.

"He isn't. He got away when they were moving him from the Scrubs in August. There was a lot about it in the papers at the time."

"I expect that's where I saw the name. You picked him up again?"

"As a matter of fact," said Petrella, "we haven't. He got across to France, and that's where he'll stop if he knows what's good for him. And if Mr Albert King should turn up looking for his property, you get in touch with your local station."

"All right," said Mr Robins. He didn't sound as if he expected it to happen.

Petrella went out into streets, which were pearly grey with mist. It was the pleasant mist of early November, which comes up from the river after a warm autumn day, and bears no resemblance to the sour London fog, which rolls in, later in the year, from the North Sea, saturated with filth and sends Londoners coughing and choking to their twilight homes.

This mist was a feathery outrider of winter, with implications of football, open fires, and hot toast; a fairy godmother of the good-natured type, who veiled all the street lamps in gauze, softened the angular austerities of brick and slate, and doubled the attraction of little, red-curtained bow windows of the pubs.

Petrella lengthened his stride, like a horse that senses the stable. If he cut through College Crescent and used the maze of connecting streets and alleys beyond, it would take him about fifteen minutes of hard walking to get back to Highside. Then home, a bath, if Mrs Catt's married daughter hadn't used up all the hot water, and a long, luxurious, leisurely evening with a book on the "Tactics of Advanced Squeeze Play" which he had bought for twopence that morning from a barrow in the Farringdon Road.

He was on the point of crossing into Q Division – he recognized the invisible boundary, because Q was his own division – when something made him check his pace very slightly, and then cross the road to the pavement on the other side. He had seen, ahead of him, a figure that he thought he recognized.

Up Carrick Street, right at the top, and into Pardoe Street. By this time he was almost certain. It was the way the man walked, with a curious lurch to the right at each step. There was no suggestion of stumbling or weakness in it. Rather the contrary, of strength and purpose, as a well-found ship will butt its way forward, with the wind across and abeam, dipping to each successive trough.

"It's Boot, all right," said Petrella to himself. "I wonder what he's up to now."

There was no real reason that he should be up to anything but there were a few men, not more, perhaps, than one or two in any division, who were automatically observed wherever they went. "Boot" Howton was one of them. As Petrella watched, he lurched rather farther than usual to the right, executed a stalling turn, and pushed open the saloon-bar door of the Punchbowl public house.

Petrella hesitated. The Punchbowl was not a pub he knew well and, inside his own manor, he was careful to drink only in the two or three houses where he knew the landlord and was known and accepted by the regulars. Then he pushed open the door marked "Private Bar. Jug and Bottle" and went in.

It was a cold, beer-smelling bulkhead in which he found himself, its sides enclosed by head-high wooden partitions, its walls and floor bare. It was furnished with one long table and one very hard bench, and was shut off from the warmth and light of the saloon bar by a row of pivoting shutters of ground glass, which added to this unpromising apartment the suggestion of an ante-room to some discreet seraglio.

However, though it had drawbacks as a place of entertainment, it formed an ideal observation post. Petrella moved one of the glass shutters a few inches and found himself looking directly into the saloon. In the foreground he had a fine view of the mirror-like seat of the landlord's trousers as he stooped to pull at a beer lever. In mid-vision was a lady with a startling carbuncle on her nose addressing herself to a glass of stout. And in the background, sure enough, was Boot Howton.

The nickname was thought to be a contraction of "Beauty", and to have been used on the well-known principle on which a twenty-stone man is called "Tiny".

Boot's face had started off some yards behind scratch, and this handicap had been increased, in early life, by the total loss of his left eye, and later by a fight in which he had been rash enough to fall down, allowing his opponent to stamp on his nose. What was left was really hardly a nose at all, more a casual accumulation of flesh in the lower middle of his face.

Boot was talking to a very tall, very thin man in a checked suit, a Cambridge-blue waistcoat and drainpipe trousers. Petrella now became aware that the landlord had turned around and was looking at him.

"A pint of mild."

"I wooden chance the mild," said the landlord.

"Bitter, then."

When it came, Petrella said, "That man in the corner with the squashed nose. He's Howton, isn't he? Do you happen to know the name of the tall man he's talking to?"

The landlord's small bright eyes flickered up and down, weighing up the strange young man in the raincoat.

"I dunno," he said. "I could ask him, I suppose."

"No. Don't do that. But see if you can find out quietly. I'd really like to know."

The landlord gave him his change, served two railwaymen who had come in on their way home off shift, and disappeared out of the bar. His place was taken by a middle-aged woman with her hair in a net.

Petrella drank his bitter slowly. If it was better than the mild, the mild must have been sensational.

The street door of the private bar swung open and Boot appeared.

"You asking for me?" he said.

Petrella awarded the landlord a black mark for treachery and himself a bigger one for stupidity.

He said, "Yes, I was."

"Orright," said Boot, coming in and slamming the door behind him. "Here I am. In person." The ghost of all the whisky he had been drinking came in with him. "You're a bogey, ent you?"

"I'm a detective sergeant."

"I heard they were getting short of recruits. I diddun realize they'd started taking 'em out of the nursery."

"Oh, that's all right," said Petrella, amiably. "I'm older than I look."

"I've a bloody good mind to give you a bloody good hiding," said Boot. He was so close that Petrella could see that his single eye was deeply bloodshot. He seemed to have some difficulty in focusing it.

Petrella was cursing his own folly. He reckoned that if it came to a pinch he was quick enough and strong enough to knock Boot down, provided none of his friends butted in. But there was neither pleasure nor profit in hitting a man who was three parts drunk.

He turned on the landlord, who was leaning over the bar, his mouth half open.

"Have you been serving this man with drink?"

The landlord gaped.

"If you have," said Petrella, "you'd better look out for your license. Can't you see he's drunk?"

"Drunk your —ing self," said Howton. He whipped up one of the bottles from the table and threw it. It missed Petrella by a clear yard, sailed onward in a lazy curve, and struck one of the square glass shutters fair in the middle. The shutter disintegrated.

"Hey!" said the landlord.

"All right," said Petrella. "Come and help put him out."

"Put out your —ing grandmother," said Howton, picking up a second bottle and swinging it. Petrella moved in under the blow, grabbed the big man by the arm six inches above his left elbow, swung him round, and, with his free hand, smacked him sharply in the small of the back. The landlord appeared through a door in the partition and grabbed his other arm expertly. As they reached the street door, it opened.

The newcomer apparently grasped the situation, for he stood smartly aside. Petrella and the landlord released their holds simultaneously, and Howton shot out into the street, staggered a few paces in an attempt to catch up with his legs, tripped, and sat down.

When he got up, the night air and the shock seemed to have driven out some of the whisky. Petrella thought he had never seen an uglier face.

"Having trouble?" inquired the newcomer, who was Detective Sergeant Gwilliam. Sergeant Gwilliam spoke in the soft accent of the valleys. There was sixteen stone of him, and he had played Rugby football for the Metropolitan Police and for Wales.

"Not really," said Petrella. "Gentleman throwing his weight about."

"He was surely doing that."

" 'Slucky for you," said Howton, fixing his single red eye on Petrella, "you've found a friend. If you'd been alone, I'd have opened you up."

He pivoted on his heel and tacked off down the street.

So Petrella and Gwilliam finished the walk home together. The mist was a little thicker now, and through it there appeared the reflected glow of flames. Something sailed through the air and exploded with a crack at their feet.

"Kids," said Gwilliam.

"Good heavens," said Petrella. "I'd forgotten. This is Guy Fawkes night, isn't it?"

"Once a year, and quite enough."

They stopped for a moment on the railway bridge and looked about them. A dozen fires were visible. The flames of the nearest leapt up, yellow and cheerful in the darkness. The light of the others was filtered by successive layers of mist from bright orange to deep rose-red. In the distance a fire-engine bell started to sound.

"Some year," said Sergeant Gwilliam, "the Fire Brigade's going on strike, and we'll wake up on November 6th and find London burned down, and serve us right."

"Oh, I don't know," said Petrella. "I think it looks rather fine."

The mixture of feathery grey with every tone of red would have ravished the eye of an artist.

"The Harringtons," he said, "have been collecting for months. They got their guy out soon after midsummer and Micky tried to stick me up for a subscription. I said, surely it isn't November yet, and Micky said 'Garn, Sarge, *this* isn't Guy Fawkes, it's Father Christmas.' "

Gwilliam grunted. He did not share Petrella's enthusiasm for the Harrington family. They walked the rest of the way to Crown Road in silence, went in under the archway, crossed the courtyard where the police wagons stood, climbed an outside iron staircase, and went through a door which badly needed a coat of paint.

On the left was the room which served Superintendent Haxtell as an office. Considering that the superintendent was responsible for all criminal investigation in a division which stretched from its southern point just above King's Cross clear up into open country between St Albans and Cheshunt and contained more than two hundred thousand inhabitants, it might seem odd that he had been provided with a room rather smaller than that occupied by a clerical civil servant of the third grade and furnished in a manner which would have brought a protest from the most junior sub-editor in Fleet Street. However, the superintendent was quite used to it. Under normal conditions he spent as little time as possible in his office.

Conditions were not normal at the moment, owing to the discovery, a week before, in an empty shed under the railway arches at Pond End, of the misused body of nine-year-old Corinne Hart. Until Corinne's killer was discovered the superintendent was tied fast to his telephone, and the tiny room was further overcrowded by the addition of a camp bed in one corner.

The room opposite was officially known as the Interview Room. Very few interviews took place in it, because most of the floor space was already occupied by filing cabinets and the rest by Detective Constable Mote's photographic apparatus.

The far end of the corridor led straight into the CID room. This looked like nothing so much as a senior classroom. It had six flat desks, each with its chair. (Normally there were only five, but the Corinne Hart inquiry had brought back Sergeant Gwilliam, temporarily, from No. 2 Station and an extra desk had to be squeezed in for him.) Petrella, as sergeant-in-charge, had the biggest desk by the window. Immediately under his eyes sat Probationary Detective Constable Wilmot. Next to him the photographic Mote. In the far corner, Detective Constable Cobley, a Devonian, known naturally as Tom. And under the second window the newly promoted Sergeant Wynne, who was by a long way the oldest man in the room but who had done all his earlier service in the colonial police and was now starting again.

There were two telephones, located on the window sill for want of anywhere better to put them, and the walls were covered with notices: sociable notices about forthcoming Christmas dances, gloomy notices about the habits of the Colorado beetle, and sharp notices starting "It has been observed that junior detective constables..." and signed "G Barstow, Detective Chief Superintendent i/c No. 2 District Metropolitan Police."

When Petrella and Gwilliam came in, this room was empty.

"Are you going to do anything about Howton?" said Gwilliam.

"I don't think so," said Petrella. "You know what they always say. 'He wasn't in uniform. I didn't know who he was. I thought he was going to hit me, so I hit him first.'"

Gwilliam grunted. "That landlord," he said. "It's in my mind that I had trouble with him before, when I was at this station. If I was you I'd tell the man on that beat to keep his eyes open. You run him in once or twice for serving drink after hours, it'll teach him to mind his manners."

"Howton's not our headache," said Petrella. "He belongs to S Division."

"I ran Howton in twice when I was in S," said Gwilliam. "He's a hard case. He and Monk Ritchie started the first Camden Town mob. Did you know? When Monk was sent up for a handful last year, Howton took over, and formed his own bunch out of what was left. Jacko, Curly, Ritzy Moritz – "

"Is Moritz very tall and thin – a fancy dresser?"

"That's right," said Gwilliam.

"Well, he was in the pub tonight," said Petrella. "Sorry. Go on."

"I was only going to say," said Gwilliam, "that I heard that when Howton took over Monk's boys he took over his Rosa at the same time. When Monk got out, we were tipped off to watch that crowd, in case Monk had got ideas of sorting things out personally. Only he never went near them. Hopped straight across to France."

Petrella said, "It's a small world, isn't it? I was checking the pawn list tonight for a piece of stuff that was meant to be part of one of Monk's jobs." There was a clatter of footsteps in the passage.

The station sergeant opened the door and said, with a grin on his face, "Three gentlemen to see you."

Petrella knew most of the boys in his manor and he recognized the leader of the deputation.

"Hullo, Ray, what's it this time?"

"We told the constable what we saw," said Ray, "and he told us to come straight along here and tell you. That's right, innit?"

The two smaller boys nodded gravely. Their faces were black with an underlayer of stove blacking and an overlayer of smoke and gunpowder and their clothes were indescribable; but they stood their ground, conscious that what they had to say would more than pay for their sins.

"Start at the beginning," said Petrella.

"We were up on Binford Sports Ground," said Ray, "getting more wood for our bonfire. The man said we could. And we found this gate. It was loose, see, and we got through."

"Which end of the sports ground?"

"The far end. Behind the running track."

"Then you must have been in the private ground round the reservoir."

" 'Sright," said Ray. "Only the gate was open – well, it was loose. So how were we to know?"

"All right," said Petrella. "You were trespassing innocently, Water Board property, looking for firewood for your bonfire. So far I'm with you. What happened next?"

"That's when we found her. A woman."

The three black faces looked up hopefully.

2

The Body of a Woman

"We'll go in the car," said Petrella.

Binford Park Reservoir was an awkward place to get at. It was wedged between the embanked main railway line on one side and the sports ground on the other. At the bottom there was an entrance from the road and a motorable track opposite the filter beds. But if they used that, it would mean waste of time getting the keys and a scramble along the steeply sloping reservoir side.

"We'll go to the sports ground," he said to the driver, "the entrance is in Carslake Road."

"What about me cushions?"

"That's all right," said Petrella. "It's their faces that are dirty, not their bottoms. Hop in, boys, and sit quiet."

They found the gates to the sports ground open and a worried little man standing beside them.

"Jackson," he said. "I'm the secretary here. I hope it's all right about those boys. There's a lot of dead wood behind the pavilion. I told them they could have that – "

"That's all right, Mr Jackson," said Petrella. "Could you hold the gate a little wider so we can get the car in."

"It's terribly muddy beyond the pavilion."

"I expect we shall manage."

They bumped off up a path which soon degenerated into a track.

"Lucky we got four-wheel drive," said the driver, nursing the heavy car skillfully. "Can't go much further without chains."

"All right. We'll walk from here. See if you can turn her round without getting bogged. I don't know what we're going to need yet."

He set off into the darkness, with the boys trotting behind him. In the middle of nowhere they stopped, sodden grass under their feet. The mist was thicker.

"Where now?"

The boys consulted, doubtfully. Petrella had an inspiration. "Did you say something about a policeman?"

"That's right," said Ray. "We found a copper, outside the gate. Showed him where to go. It wasn't so thick, then."

"That's all right, then," said Petrella, "he ought to hear us if we shout altogether. Oy!"

Two trebles and one busted treble joined the chorus. A faint shout answered them. They turned to their left and started to climb toward it. Soon the ground levelled out and their feet crunched on a cinder track. Then down again, sharply, toward an iron fence. The shout came again, to their left, and much nearer.

They found Police Constable Farrer standing by the gate.

"Wotter night," he said. "Oh, it's you, Sergeant. Here she is. Lock's busted. You push her and she'll open. I took one look inside to see they weren't making it all up, then I came out."

"Quite right," said Petrella. He switched on his big torch. The gate was no more than a section of the rusty iron fence, which had been equipped in ages long past, with hinges on one side and a lock on the other. It was so long since it had been used that the path beyond, straight down through the bushes, was now hardly visible.

"Halfway down on the left, in the bushes, just off the path, if you can call it a path," said Farrer. "Been there some time, I'd say."

The lock of the gate had rusted and snapped. Petrella pushed against the resisting weed and grass beyond and squeezed through the gap. He kept, as much as he could, to the side of the path, but it wasn't easy in that sloping, sodden wilderness. Every time he felt his feet slipping he remembered that the reservoir was immediately below him. He found her easily enough. He saw what must have caught the boys' eyes earlier in the evening. The sole of a brown shoe, set at that unmistakable angle which means, at once, that the shoe is not a derelict cast-off but is attached to a human body.

She was lying on a shelf of earth which ran parallel with the bank of the reservoir and about halfway up the slope. It was an exaggeration to say that she was buried. She was lying in a slight dip, and the grass had grown round her and the leaves had blown over her.

If she had been a yard or two further in from the path, he thought, she might have lain there until the Day of Judgement, when all hearts are opened.

Petrella switched off his torch and climbed slowly back to the top of the bank. He had a decision to make. Clearly there was nothing to be done before morning. In fact, trampling round in the dark they might already have done more harm than good. On the other hand, even in cases of this sort, to waste no time was the inflexible rule. He had worked things out by the time he had got through the gate and heaved it shut behind him.

"There's no sense in you staying on guard, Farrer," he said. "There's nothing to guard against, and all you'll catch will be double pneumonia. Get the station to send a man up at first light. One man should do. There's no need to make a lot of fuss. I don't suppose we should get many people up here anyway."

This reminded him of something else. He turned to the boys, who were standing in a row like sparrows hopeful of further crumbs from a promising feast.

"I'll get the driver to take you home," he said. "Your mothers and fathers will want to know what you've been up to. Well, you can tell 'em – tell 'em everything – except where the body is. If we have a crowd up here first thing tomorrow, I'll know who's to blame and I'll come after you with a belt."

Ray exposed his gap teeth in a beautiful smile. His prestige was going to be so heightened by his return home in a police car that nothing else mattered.

"I won't tellum," he said.

Having got rid of his assistants, Petrella had a word with the anxious man at the main gate, the resident secretary of the Sports Club.

"Of course you can use our telephone, Sergeant," he said. "As a matter of fact, my wife's just making a cup of tea."

Petrella got through to Superintendent Haxtell. He kept it short. He knew that the superintendent's mind was fully occupied with the elaborate campaign which had now spread outward from the empty railway shed under the arches and embraced two whole postal districts, and in which hundreds of men had already asked questions of tens of thousands of people and would question tens of thousands more.

"There's nothing to suggest murder," he concluded apologetically. "It could easily be suicide – or natural causes, even. But I thought – "

"Quite right," said Haxtell. "Always cater for the worst, first. I'll get a pathologist up to you in the morning. You can manage all the rest of it?"

"I'm staying on the spot," said Petrella, "and I'll go up there myself at first light."

"Fine," said Haxtell, and ran off.

Mr Jackson, who had come in with the cup of tea, said, "If you'd care to use our spare bed, we'd be only too pleased. And we could lend you an alarm clock."

It seemed no more than a slow count of ten after his head had touched the pillow that the shrill bell jerked Petrella back to life. He quelled the clock before it would wake his host and hostess, got out of bed, and padded across to the window.

The mist was gone and stars were showing in a clear sky. Morning was not far off.

Ten minutes later he was easing open the rusted iron gate, which squeaked protestingly. This time he avoided the path

15

altogether, making his way along the inside of the iron railing, and then forcing his way down, where the undergrowth looked thinnest, until he stood on the path which ran round the reservoir.

The place was alive with birds. There were swans, grebes, and coots on the water, along with ducks of all shapes and sizes; and the trees and bushes around him were full of birds, singing their morning songs. Petrella wondered how many Londoners passed that spot every day without having any idea of the existence of this hidden sheet of water.

But his mind was running on something besides birds. A policeman's memory is a scrapbook and pasted into it are a thousand disconnected cuttings. Things seen. Things heard. Things read. And somewhere in it, tucked away in an unimportant corner, was something about that very reservoir. Something quite recent. Something in the papers – ?

A swan with a black cap on its head and a face like an elderly barrister arose suddenly from the rushes on the left and hissed at him. Petrella continued circumspectly on his way and eventually made the complete circuit of the water and climbed back to the field.

Full light brought up a uniformed reinforcement; and Dr Summerson, and Dr Summerson's secretary. Petrella watched them cross the running track.

Dr Summerson was leading, his hands in his raincoat pockets, his black Homburg on the back of his head. Petrella had seen him at work in some fairly gruesome and some fairly outlandish circumstances and had never known him other than composed, alert, and freshly shaved. There was a theory in police circles that he carried an electric razor in his car and shaved as he drove.

"Morning, Sergeant. Petrella, isn't it? An assault case on Helenwood Common last March? Right? I thought I recognized you. Now, how do you want me to get at this one?"

"I thought we'd better keep off the path as much as possible, sir. I've found a way down to the water. Then we can come up at her from below."

"Fine. Let's have the bag, Milly. And look out for your nylons."

"If I wore nylons on these trips," said Milly, "I'd soon be broke."

Petrella showed them the place, and then wandered off on another complete circuit of the water. It was light enough to see more detail now. The track ran round the long western and the short northern sides of the reservoir at water level and then turned onto the crown of a grassy causeway which separated the eastern side of the reservoir from the New River that fed it. At the southern end the ground opened out. There was a small, yellow-brick and grey-slate cottage, which looked deserted. Beyond the cottage the track became a cinder-covered road, wide enough for a car. Petrella followed it down to the main-road gate, which was locked. On the other side of the main road, he seemed to remember, lay the filter beds and pumping stations and other centres of activity.

He went back to the cottage. There were curtains in the windows, but it had a cold, dead look. He knocked, and knocked again, but got no reply. When he looked up he saw that he was being watched by a large brown rat, which winked at him and vanished into the tangled mass of what had once been a kitchen garden.

He completed his second circuit and found Dr Summerson finishing off.

"I'll give you enough to be getting on with," he said. "Hold those scissors a moment, Milly. Right?"

Petrella opened his notebook at a clean page and nodded.

"Woman of about thirty-five. Well, say middle thirties. Black hair. Difficult to be sure what she looked like – the face, I mean."

Petrella raised his eyes, then averted them hastily.

"Taken good care of her figure. No surplus fat. I think it'd be safe to guess that she was a nice-looking woman. Used heavy make-up, anyway. Clothes good, but I wouldn't say West End, would you, Milly?"

His secretary paused for a moment from repairing her own good-looking face to say, "Upper-class prices, lower middle-class taste."

"You'll get a lot more detail out of the clothes when the laboratory's had a go at them. There's a maker's label in the back of the dress which is too stained to read, but those boys will be able to make it out for sure." Summerson paused, and added, "Dead one to two months. That's only a guess at the moment. I'll try and close the bracket a bit when I do the autopsy."

"Was she – ?" Petrella hesitated.

"Go on," said Summerson. "Ask it. They always do. Was she murdered? I haven't the faintest idea. When I've finished the autopsy I may be able to guess. But I'm not going to jump the gun. That's a thing I *have* learnt. One of my first cases for the police. A boy, in Essex, found hanging in a farmyard. Symptoms of strangulation, rope mark round his neck. No one had any doubt it was suicide. That afternoon I was doing the PM in the Epping Mortuary. The man in charge of the case – it was Chief Inspector Glaister – that was in the days before they made 'em all super-intendents – was watching me do it. He'd just said, 'I wonder what a nice boy like that would be thinking of to hang himself – ' when something rolled out of him and fell on the floor with a clatter. Do you know what it was? – it was a bloody great forty-five revolver bullet. I'm sure I've told you this story before, Milly."

"Last time it was a Luger."

"What a memory," said Summerson coldly. "Just hold that plastic bag while I shovel this in, will you?"

While they were finishing off, Petrella had a word with the constable.

"I can't see any of the reservoir people moving yet," he said. "But they're bound to appear soon. If they notice you, just tell 'em what it's about and warn them to keep off. If they don't notice you, so much the better. I'll have to tell the Water Board about it, of course, but I'd rather do it on my own time. By the way, have you had any breakfast yet?"

"A cupper before I came out. Nothing else."

Petrella looked at his watch. It was still short of eight o'clock. A lot seemed to have happened already that day.

"I'll get a relief up," he said. "By nine o'clock. You won't die of starvation before then."

Summerson gave Petrella a lift back to Crown Road Police Station. He drove very well and very fast.

"You won't get an ambulance up that field," said Petrella to the station sergeant. "Better send it in through the main-road gate. Then a stretcher party along the edge of the reservoir. It'll be easier to move the body down than up. I'll go with them and show them the place."

Then there were the arrangements to make for relieving the constable. And a very quick report to scribble for his superior officer. And it suddenly occurred to Petrella that he hadn't had any breakfast either; and that the possibility of having any was receding. He took down a telephone directory and looked up the number of the Metropolitan Water Board.

Superintendent Haxtell read Petrella's report at ten o'clock. He read it furtively, holding it under the table, because he was at a conference. It was one of an apparently interminable series of conferences. He sometimes thought that if they moved about a bit more and talked a bit less their chances of nailing Corinne Hart's killer would be improved.

Detective Chief Superintendent Barstow was in the chair. He was a big, red-faced man, with a powerful nose and a strong digestion. He was in charge of Criminal Investigation in No. 2 District, which covers North London and is the largest, in both population and area, of the four Metropolitan Police Districts. He was Haxtell's immediate superior and was one of the reasons why Haxtell sometimes thought of taking up poultry farming.

"Let's put it this way," said Barstow. "You're morally sure that Hunt's the man but you can't prove it yet."

Haxtell considered carefully. Opinions incautiously uttered had sometimes been used against him afterwards.

"I'm sure, myself, that Hunt did it," he said. "I'm equally sure that the evidence we've so far got wouldn't stand up in court."

"Then get some more," said Barstow. He said things like that, Haxtell thought, quite automatically. Just as a certain type of army sergeant would say, "You're not paid to think."

"It isn't only a matter of not having evidence against him," he said. "There's positive evidence on the other side. His mother's covering up for him. She's prepared to swear that he was at home all evening."

"You'd be surprised," said the grey-haired man at the other side of the table, "how many sex-killers turn out to be their mother's favourite sons."

"You trick cyclists!" said Barstow. "Because a boy wets his bed he'll grow up into a cat burglar. I'm afraid I don't believe in that stuff."

"What *do* you believe in, then?" asked the psychiatrist politely. "Original sin?"

"I think we may be able to break the mother's story down," said Haxtell, before the row could develop. "There's no doubt Hunt *was* out that night. And somewhere in this area." He demonstrated on the map a half-mile square which embraced twenty or thirty little streets. "We're going through all that again. Pedestrians, motorists, householders – "

"That's the form," said Barstow. That was police work as he understood it. He peered at the map. "What's that up at the north end?" he said. "Looks like a lot of fish ponds."

"That's the Binford Park Reservoir," Haxtell said. "Actually what you're looking at's the filter beds. The reservoir itself is tucked away on the north of the road."

"Tucked away is right," said Barstow. "I thought I knew that area quite well, but I'd no idea it was there."

"Which reminds me," said Haxtell. He got out the notes. "We found a body there last night. It's been there some time."

He told the story briefly.

20

"It could be natural causes – suicide – murder. Until we get Summerson's report we won't know. Been there since September. The real difficulty is to know who to put on to it."

Barstow considered. In addition to Superintendent Haxtell he should, by rights, have had three detective chief inspectors under him, but owing to shortages elsewhere he was reduced to two. And one of them, Manifold, had been sent, dead against his wishes, on a three months' attachment in America; which left Gover from No. 3 Station. Probably Gover was overworked too. Who wasn't?

"Give it to Gover," he said, "and send him a sergeant to do the actual work. Who've you got?"

"Petrella found the body."

Barstow considered. He could think of nothing actually against Petrella.

"As long as he's got a senior man with him and does what he's told and doesn't go running off on his own."

"I think he's got more sense of responsibility now."

"He's learning," conceded Barstow. "The only trouble with that young man is that he thinks he'll be assistant commissioner one day."

"Psychologically speaking," said the doctor, "that's the best way to become assistant commissioner." Like all good psychiatrists, he was a patient man, and he had been waiting to get one back at Barstow.

3

Bird Life and Back Numbers

Unaware that his character was under discussion, Petrella was making his way by bus to the neighbouring suburb of Hounds Green to interview an authority called the resident supply engineer of the Metropolitan Water Board. There he tracked down Mr Lundgren, whom he found in a pleasant office, seated under a picture of one of the bearded heroes who had constructed the New River two centuries before, thus assuring London of the best water supply of any capital in the world.

"What's all this?" he said. "A body, on the bank, eh? Get plenty of them in the river, poor souls. The gratesmen are always pulling them out. But I'm not surprised, all the same. They're isolated places, those reservoirs."

"I've walked past this one a dozen times," agreed Petrella, "without having any idea it was there. The railway embankment hides it altogether on one side."

"You ought to run up to Cheshunt sometime," said Mr Lundgren. "Go along the New Cambridge arterial road *with* a map and see if you can spot the South Reservoir. A perfect piece of natural camouflage. I doubt if anyone, except a few anglers or bird watchers, sets foot in it from year to year."

"I saw a lot of birds on this reservoir," said Petrella. "There was a swan which sounded as if it had got whooping cough."

"Quite right. That's a whooper. When I retire I'm going to write a book. *Bird Life on Our London Reservoirs.* They're not only water birds either. Woodpeckers of all sorts, and golden orioles. Three years ago" – Mr Lundgren tried vainly to keep the pride out of his voice – "we had a northern diver. One of three confirmed appearances so far south of the Wash. As a matter of fact, I spotted him myself."

"Goodness!" said Petrella.

"I mustn't waste your time. What can I do for you?"

"Could you tell whoever's in charge on the spot what we're up to?"

"The reservoir foreman. Yes, I'll tell him. It doesn't look as if he's spotted you yet or I should have heard about it."

"There's no reason he should," said Petrella. "We're in the trees and bushes, on the west bank. And we got in by the running track. There's a gate there, by the way, needs mending. Looks as if it's been broken for some time."

Mr Lundgren made a note.

"We shall want to bring an ambulance in by the main gate. We can get it as far as the cottage. Then we'll do the rest of the trip with a stretcher. There's no one living in the cottage, is there?"

"That's right. It belongs to the intake attendant. He's what you might call the resident caretaker of the reservoir. The cottage goes with the job."

"Of course!" said Petrella, deeply relieved. "Oh, I'm sorry. It's only that I just remembered something that's been bothering me. You know how you think of a thing. And then you can't remember what it was. Haven't you been advertising for a new – what do you call it – intake attendant?"

"That's right. For about two months. In *The Times* and in the *North London Press.*"

"I wouldn't have thought you'd have much difficulty, with a cottage thrown in. To say nothing of all those birds."

"Time was," said Lundgren, "we didn't need to advertise. We'd got a waiting list. In the present state of the labour market – well, you can see for yourself. It's taken two months to get three suitable candidates. We have to be a bit fussy on our side too. It's not a difficult job, but it needs a conscientious sort of bloke. And there's the health angle."

"What happened to the last one?"

"Ricketts. He walked out on us. Said it was too quiet at night. He's gone to Blackpool."

"I expect it was the whooper swan got him down in the end," said Petrella.

He gobbled some lunch on the way back to Crown Road. In the CID room he found Inspector Gover waiting for him and learned that he had got a new boss. Nothing could have pleased him more. Gover looked like a sales manager. He had served a long apprenticeship in the Company Fraud Department and it was not until he had gone out on an emergency call with the Flying Squad and had himself arrested and held an armed warehouse breaker that it had occurred to his superiors that he was anything more than a conscientious clerk. Petrella had worked under him many times and knew him for a quiet, determined, even-tempered person.

When Gover had heard Petrella out, he said, "You'd better get back and have a look round. See what you can pick up. Contact the men working at the reservoir. They may have some ideas. I'll let you know just as soon as we get Summerson's report. We're all really waiting on that."

As Petrella was going, he added, "And take a padlock and chain with you for that broken gate. Then we needn't keep a man up there. Now that the body's gone, he's probably attracting more attention than he's doing good."

Petrella found a bored constable sitting on his cape. The running track had not been used, and no one had come near him from the public side. One of the Water Board men had started to come up through the bushes, but he had shouted to him to keep clear.

"Funny old place, isn't it?" said the constable. "You wouldn't hardly know it was there."

"That's right," said Petrella. "The forgotten continent." He snapped the padlock home, and started to climb down the slope through the bushes. "If I'm not back by the end of the month, send a search party."

The constable grinned, and Petrella, not looking where he was going, slid the last ten feet and landed on his bottom on the path. The water lay like quicksilver under the quiet afternoon sun.

On the far bank two men were working with rakes. He made his way slowly round toward them, stopping again to look at the little cottage at the southern end. He pictured it in the depths of winter, with the rain beating down and the wind whistling round its chimneys. Or in a fog. Perhaps there was something to be said for Blackpool after all.

At the foot of the overgrown patch of vegetable garden was a small landing stage and on the left of the landing stage a boat shed. It was just a canopy on piles, open on three sides and big enough to shelter a dinghy. There was no sign of any boat.

Now the two men were walking toward him. Petrella went to meet them. They introduced themselves as the foreman and one of the walks-men. He found himself learning something about the little kingdom of the reservoir.

The foreman was the boss. Under him he had two watermen, who cleared grates and cut weeds and looked after the sluices; and two walks-men, who, in turns, walked sentry along the banks of the New River and saw that nothing occurred to pollute or disturb the main sources of London water. All four men lived in cottages outside the main-road gate.

"We oughter have one more," said the foreman.

"An intake attendant," said Petrella proudly. "It's all right. That's not a fluke. I've been talking to your Mr Lundgren."

"Ah!" said the foreman. "An intake attendant. There's not much to the job. But it's handy to have someone on the spot at nights."

"A nice steady job?"

"That's right. Ricketts – now, he was here more than two years. Nearer three, wasn't it?"

The walks-man said he thought Ricketts had been there three years, but time went by so fast it was hard to tell.

"Then, suddenly, one day, out he goes. That's the way it always happens."

Petrella asked the foreman if he was much troubled by trespassers. The foreman had never known such a thing. Nor had the walks-man. "We got railway on one side," he said. "Main line to the North. *Scotsman*'s just about due, isn't she? And it's not just the railway line. There's a long row of engine sheds, you see, and maintenance workshops the other side. You couldn't get through that way without you did a lot of climbing."

"What about the sports ground?"

"Them?" said the foreman. "They're so busy running four-minute miles they don't know we're here, do they, Sam? Here she comes!"

They stood and watched the great green-and-gold monster hurl itself along the embanked line and disappear with a scream into Hounds Green high-level tunnel.

"Well, keep your eyes open," said Petrella. "And if you see anything – " He gave them his name and telephone number.

Then he walked back to the path and climbed carefully up alongside it. The passage of time, and the work of removing the body, had made it highly unlikely that anything useful could be picked up. But he searched all the same, patiently and carefully. What a detective really needed was a telescopic neck; or eyes on stalks, like a crab.

His only find of the slightest interest was a folded copy of the *Evening Standard* under a bush, beside where the body had lain. The date was Saturday, September 22nd, which tied in well enough with Summerson's guess. Near enough seven weeks. He folded it carefully and put it in his raincoat pocket.

A voice was calling him from the top. It was Detective Constable Mote.

"Could you come, quickly?" he said. "I've got the car down by the pavilion."

"What's up?" said Petrella.

"Inspector Gover wants you," said Mote. "He's got the report."

"What's in it?"

"Search me," said Mote, "but since he told me to get you back as fast as I bloody well could I don't imagine it's natural causes."

Dr Summerson's report was brief and to the point.

"This woman," it concluded, "was shot, probably at very close quarters, possibly with the muzzle of the gun pressed up against her body. The bullet lodged high up in the spinal cord. Death would have been instantaneous. It is suggested that unless the gun comes to light within a few feet of the body any question of suicide can be ruled out. Further, some of the leaves, leaf deposit, and mold which was covering the body appears, on further examination, to be several years old at least. If it proves, on re-examination, to be so, it is clear that the body was covered after death. I have submitted these vegetation samples and shoes and clothing to the Forensic Science Laboratory for detailed examination. The woman was three months pregnant. So far there are no indications of identity. A more detailed report will follow."

"Identity," said Gover. Identity, the first and sometimes the only problem. Who was she? How had someone, some living, breathing, talking person, with friends and relations, with lawyer and doctor, with landlord, greengrocer, and milkman, dropped quietly out, like a cockroach through a crack in the floorboards and no voices raised to protest the disappearance? What sort of human unit was it that its departure left no gap at all in the pattern?

"Missing persons lists," said Gover. "Try them first. Get the main list from Central. She may not be a local woman. Description for circulation. It won't be a good one, but it's better than nothing. And we'll take a chance on it, and say that she died on – what was the date on that paper? – September 22nd. That's the sort of thing people *do* remember. Next, clothes. We'll have to wait for that. If you tell the laboratory that something's urgent, they start talking about 'Science can't be rushed' and take twice as long. Still, one good laundry mark might solve all our problems."

"Summerson did say that there was a shop label in the dress and that it ought to be legible. I didn't build on it, much, because according to his secretary it's a sort of wholesale model – not an exclusive little number run up for madame only."

"Let's wait and see," said Gover. "Shoes the same. Now what about teeth?" He turned back to the beginning of the report. "She seems to have looked after them pretty well – dash her. No plate, no dentures, not even a gold cap. A few stoppings. That's not going to help until we know who she is, and then we probably shan't need them."

"Fingerprints."

"Have a word with Blinder. It's probably not too late to get decent prints. They're quite clever at that sort of thing now. But unless she's got a record they're not going to be much use at this stage. Anything else?"

"Someone had better look after my routine stuff for a day or two," said Petrella diffidently. "And can I have one man to help? I'd like Mote. He's handy with a camera."

"All right," said Gover. "That's reasonable. I'll square it with the superintendent. You get on down to Central."

Detective Sergeant Blinder was a large, sad, dedicated man who worked in the Fingerprint Section at New Scotland Yard. The Fingerprint Section is, in theory, an annexe to the Criminal Record Office, but as the fingerprint records pour in, thousand upon thousand from all parts of the country and from almost every part of the world, so has the annexe grown until, like the cuckoo, it threatens to oust its co-tenants. Sergeant Blinder sometimes foresaw, with gloomy satisfaction, the time when the rest of Scotland Yard would be a mere annexe to the Fingerprint Section.

Petrella found him studying a ten-magnification enlargement of a thumbprint, and put his problems to him.

"Six weeks? Certainly, we'll get a nice set of prints. Unless the rats – "

Petrella said that he hadn't seen any sign of rats.

"Why, the other day," said Sergeant Blinder, "they brought us a girl, been nine weeks in the water. *In the water,* I'm telling you."

Petrella nodded. Fragments of Sergeant Blinder's discourse reached him. "Skin nearly detached – paraffin wax injection – made a mold – lovely job." He was wondering, not for the first time, in just what curious vacuums of their own creation the scientific branches of the CID existed. Did their minds ever relate the detached fragments of skin and bone, of tissue and adipocere, to the living creatures of which they had once formed part, creatures with desires and fears and Schedule A tax? Was it lack of sensibility or was it merely the protective armament of habit?

"Two inverted arches and a characteristic delta," concluded the sergeant triumphantly.

"You'd be able to tell me if you had a record of this girl?"

"Give me four clear prints off one hand and I'll tell you in a couple of minutes. Single prints – well, that's more difficult."

"You shall have both hands," said Petrella, and made his escape.

There were other things to do. There were the missing persons lists to check, not very hopefully. He had a few details of height and supposed weight and age, but not really enough. "Give us a mole on the chin or a squint in the left eye, and maybe we can help you," said the clerkly Inspector East, who presided over these mysteries. "When relatives report a missing person they don't say, 'She was five foot six and a half inches high and approximately nine stone in weight' – they say, 'She'd got a cleft palate, Inspector, and Lord, didn't she spit when she talked.' "

Petrella laughed. "We may be able to do better later on," he said. "If you could keep a general eye open for any woman who went missing in the last fortnight of September."

Inspector East promised that he would do what he could.

The mention of the last fortnight in September put Petrella in mind of something else. He felt in his pocket and pulled out the carefully folded copy of the *Evening Standard.* There was something he had meant to check.

"Bit out of date, aren't you?" said the inspector, looking over his shoulder. "I've got a midday edition if you'd care to borrow it."

"This is something I picked up near the body," said Petrella. "I thought so – you see? The middle sheet is missing. It goes straight from page ten to page fifteen. I wonder what was on it."

"Short of seeing the missing page, I don't know how you're going to find out."

"I might do that, too," said Petrella.

Outside it was dark and a thin drizzle of rain was falling. He took a bus along the Embankment and walked the short distance up Farringdon Road, pushing into the tide of home-going office workers, heads down, umbrellas up, individually insignificant, potent in mass as a lemming migration.

The *Standard,* being an evening paper, observes rational hours, but Petrella found the back numbers department still open, and introduced himself.

"Do what we can," said the man. "Any particular edition?"

"This one calls itself a late night final."

"On the streets about three o'clock. Hold on a minute."

The man disappeared. Petrella waited. A boy of the type bred only by London newspaper offices wandered in, whistling; kicked the wainscoting three or four times as if he was getting his own back on life, and wandered out again. Then the man reappeared.

"Bit short on that edition," he said, "but I found one for you."

Petrella spread it out on the table. The middle sheet was made up of pictures and news items. The passage of six weeks had given most of them a curiously dated look. "Test cricketer in car smash." In September a test cricketer was still news. By

November he could kill himself and the papers would take no notice.

What he wanted was tucked away in the bottom corner of the page.

POLICE SEARCH FOR JAIL BREAKER

"Chris ('Monk') Ritchie escaped yesterday in transit from Wormwood Scrubs, where he had been serving the first weeks of a five-year sentence, to a permanent prison at Parkhurst. He slipped the handcuff attaching him to the warder, Seldon, who was conducting him, knocked down another warder, ran the length of the coach, and jumped from the moving train. London gangster Ritchie received his sentence for breaking and entering and violence. He is five foot nine, heavily built, with dark hair and face, and has a scar running from the corner of his right eye to the corner of his mouth. Police are watching his known haunts, including his flat where his wife Rosa still lives."

(Petrella smiled at this careful indiscretion.)

"Note for those interested. 'Monk' is thought to be short for 'monkey'. Ritchie once performed as part of a two-man trapeze act in a circus. He certainly showed some of his old skill when he exited from that train yesterday!"

Petrella folded the paper carefully, thanked the man, and went outside. It had stopped raining. He thought he would walk some of the way home. He found that his mind worked better if he kept moving. And here was something to think about.

For the first time in this tangle of loose ends, in this case which was not yet a case, an outline had appeared; a tiny, but identifiable outline which had shown itself for a moment before dislimning and fading back into the surrounding obscurity.

For Petrella had given evidence at Monk Ritchie's trial; and Monk's wife, Rosa, had been there and been pointed out to him.

31

A pleasant, dark-haired woman of about thirty-five. He had remembered feeling sorry for her.

4

The King of Nowhere

"Well, it could be Rosa Ritchie," agreed Gover. "But it's not going to be easy to get an identification. Not after all that time in the open."

"Fingerprints?"

"Had she got a record? I never heard of it."

"Clothes? Teeth?"

"Teeth would be best. Or you might pick up a print or two from her flat. Have you located that yet?"

"It's a couple of rooms in Corum Street. I haven't had time to go down there yet. The trouble is, she wasn't living alone, she shared with another girl. Who's probably relet them by now."

"But if Rosa didn't turn up one evening, why didn't the other girl report – " Gover stopped. "No, of course. If she shared rooms with Rosa she'd know about her private life. She'd assume Rosa had gone across to France with her husband."

"Which she may have done."

"She didn't go *with* him," said Gover. He waited for a moment or two while his careful mind sorted it all out.

"Monk – if it was Monk – crossed alone. He left Victoria by the night train. There was a bad slip-up over that. A very bad slip. The stopper wasn't put on at Newhaven until the next morning. Someone lost his job over that. But that didn't bring Monk back. A railway detective and a customs man both swear it was Monk. He wasn't disguised."

"He took a risk."

"Well, it came off. That's the thing about risks. If they come off, they're good ones. And we checked the tickets. There was one return ticket, bought over the counter, for cash, that day at a big travel agency in the Strand. The outward half was used, the inward half's never been handed in. Which means that *someone* went to France six weeks ago and hasn't come back yet."

"If it was Monk, why take a return?"

"If you're pretending to be a tourist, what else would you take?" Gover paused again. "It's not conclusive, I agree. The ticket's valid for three months. The owner may still turn out to be an absent-minded professor, with friends in Paris. All the same, I think it was Monk."

"Yes," said Petrella.

"But I don't think he took Rosa with him. And what's more, I don't think he meant to. He had to see her. She was his banker. She'd got all his money. Money she'd been slowly realizing from the proceeds of his jewel thefts, which they'd stowed away somewhere."

"Yes," said Petrella. Another tiny little piece fell into place. "But why would he meet her beside a reservoir in North London?"

"I've no idea," said Gover. "And you ought to know better than to ask. You can't answer detailed questions at this stage. All we can get at is the outline. Anyway – they do meet there. And they quarrel. And he shoots her. Now why would he do that?"

Petrella said, "Because she wanted to go with him. And it didn't fit in with his plans."

"Or because he'd heard that she'd been carrying on with his Number Two, Boot Howton?"

"Or because she didn't produce enough money, and he thought she'd been cheating him?"

"Or for all three reasons. Or for no reason at all. A man like Monk, fresh out of prison, no sleep for two days, a gun in his hand. He wouldn't want a lot of reason, would he?"

Petrella agreed. It had been a constant surprise to him, the totally inadequate reasons for which people killed other people.

"There are two ways of getting at this," said Gover. "I'm assuming, for the moment, that the woman is Rosa. We can plug away at the girl who shared the flat – what's her name, by the way?"

"A Mrs Jean Fraser."

"Well, you can look after her. You're the right age for girls. Then there's Boot and the boys. Monk must have made contact with them after he got out, don't you think? He had to get the gun from somewhere. I'd better have a word with them."

"You don't think," said Petrella, "that we'd better swap jobs. You take Jean, and leave the boys to me?"

"Certainly not," said Gover. "I'm a quiet man. I'll take the safe job. But you might see if you can find out for me where they hang out."

Next morning Petrella did some telephoning and managed to catch Detective Sergeant Luard of S Division. Bill Luard, a Cornishman, had occupied the next-door cubicle to Petrella at recruit training school, and they had liked each other and had kept up with each other, as far as their jobs allowed.

This was a piece of luck for Petrella, since detective officers are normally as jealous as tipsters of their private contacts and sources of information.

"See you tonight, when I come off duty," said Luard. "The room over Pino's at King's Cross. Remember, I took you there once? Don't get there before eight. If I'm not there, wait *outside*."

At a quarter past eight, Petrella hopped off the trolley bus at the stop under the arch and took his bearings.

Pino's lay at the blind end of Hope Street. It had net curtains in the windows. One step down from the pavement brought you into a room with two cross-legged bamboo tables, a counter and a tea urn. Not even the oldest regular could remember anyone ever being served from the tea urn, which was thought to be strictly for ornament. Upstairs there was a larger room and this was apt to be full at all hours of the day, for Pino, who derived his name from his birthplace in the Philippine Islands, brewed strong tea and excellent coffee, and his wife, who was as black as he was, was a good cook.

When Petrella poked his head round the door, all conversation ceased until Luard spotted him, jumped to his feet, and came across. Then the conversation switched on again where it had left off. For Pino's was a club, and in its way as exclusive as the Athenaeum. More so, really. It might have tolerated a bishop, but no Conservative Member of Parliament would have got past the tea urn.

"Come on," said Luard. "Coffee, Pino. Let's take this table, then we can talk." Two men in oily denim overalls got up and said they were going anyway, and Petrella squeezed in onto the wooden bench beside Luard.

"What are you up to now, Patrick?"

Petrella explained, as well as he could, uneasily aware that an old woman in black was drinking in every word he said.

"Don't worry about Kate. She's deaf," said Luard. "Aren't you?" he bellowed suddenly. The old woman bobbed and smiled.

"I can give you what you want. In fact, I'll be glad to. It's about time those boys were shaken down. They've been getting too big for their boots lately. You know it used to be Monk Ritchie's crowd. When he and Meister ran it, it was almost respectable. Housebreaking, shopbreaking. That sort of thing."

It didn't sound very respectable, but Petrella knew what Luard meant.

"Now Meister's gone up for that banknote job and Monk's out of the country, Boot Howton's taken it over. It's a real shower now, I promise you."

"Intimidation?"

"I suppose you could call stamping on people's faces intimidation," agreed Luard. "Here comes the coffee."

"Who else is in it? Ritzy Moritz I've met."

"It varies. The main characters are Moritz, Jacko and 'Curly' Thompson. Howton runs it. He's the one that makes it tick. When he goes down – and that can't be too soon as far as we're concerned – it'll fall to the ground."

"Until someone picks it up again," said Petrella. Criminals were part of his job, but criminals like Howton and Moritz and Jacko filled his soul with the weariness of deep disgust. Corner boys of crime, men without any purpose beyond making money and avoiding work, men who lived from prison sentence to prison sentence, causing the maximum of trouble, inside and outside, and doing no good to anyone, least of all to themselves.

" – enjoyed your coffee?" said Luard.

"It's first class," said Petrella. "I'm sorry, I was just thinking. Where do they hang out now?"

"You'll find them, any evening, in the back room of a pub called the King of Nowhere."

"King of Nowhere?"

"In Parrock Street, Camden Town. Got a back entrance on the canal, so I'm told. You want to watch that when you go after them."

"I'll tell Gover about it," said Petrella.

"Nothing to do with me, really," said Luard. "But what's it all about?"

"You remember that woman we found up on the reservoir?"

"Yes. I saw something about it. Suicide, wasn't it?"

"It wasn't suicide," said Petrella. "And it could be Rosa Ritchie – Monk's wife. We're not sure yet."

Luard whistled as he worked out the implications of this.

"What do you think?" he said. "Did Monk knock her off, because she'd been going with Howton, or did Howton and the boys knock her off to stop her telling Monk what she'd been up to, or did they all do it together, because her accounts wouldn't add up?"

"We'd thought of all those," said Petrella. "And it could be any of them. But, since Monk's not available, we've got to get what we can out of his friends."

"The only way you'll get anything out of them's with a big sharp tin opener," said Luard. "You'll have to excuse me now. My boyfriend's turned up."

Petrella saw a little man looking round the edge of the door and guessed that it would be the informer whom Luard had arranged to meet.

"Thanks for everything," he said. "Can I pay for my coffee?"

"It's on the house."

"Oyez, oyez, oyez," said the Highside coroner's officer severely, addressing himself to an audience which consisted of Inspector Gover, Dr Summerson, Detective Sergeant Petrella, Sergeant Oddson, a junior reporter from the *Highside Mercury,* and an old man connected with the next case. "All manner of persons who have anything to do before the queen's coroner for this borough draw near and give your attendance."

Everyone sat down. The Highside coroner, Mr Pearly, a twinkling little man, his natural gaiety undimmed by twenty years of looking upon death, nodded to his old friend Dr Summerson and waved to his officer, who whisked Sergeant Oddson into the box where he told the court that he was a Detective Sergeant in the Photographic Section at New Scotland Yard and that he wished to produce and identify four photographs, two general photographs of the Binford Park Reservoir and two of a body recently found there.

The coroner examined the photographs closely and said he thought they were very good. Sergeant Oddson looked gratified and made way for Dr Summerson.

The coroner, seeing him in the box, apparently forgot that he had waved to him a short time before and said, in tones of deep surprise, "You are Ian Monteith Summerson, a registered medical practitioner and a pathologist at Greys Hospital?"

Dr Summerson admitted that he was.

"And you performed an autopsy upon the deceased woman?"

Dr Summerson admitted this, too.

"All I shall ask you, at this juncture, Dr Summerson, is the cause of death."

"The cause of death," said Dr Summerson, "was a revolver bullet of .455 caliber, fired at very close range, which entered the base of the heart bag, and lodged in the spinal column."

The single reporter nearly swallowed the rubber off the end of his pencil as it dawned on him that he was in possession of an exclusive and undoubted scoop. A lot of people had known about the discovery of a woman at the reservoir but it had been generally supposed that she had died of exposure.

He bolted for the door, collecting a disapproving glance from the coroner's officer as he went.

Gover was already in the box.

"You are Charles Gover, a detective chief inspector in Q Division and you are in charge of the police inquiries into this case?"

"That's right, sir."

"Have you concluded your inquiries?"

"No, sir."

"I understand that it will assist you if I adjourn this case."

"Yes, sir."

Mr Pearly looked round happily at the clean coloured glass of the windows, at the polished woodwork, at the spotless tiles of the floor, at the gleaming brass of the handrail in front of him, and addressed the empty benches in exactly the same courteous, dispassionate tones that he would have used had they been full, as they sometimes were, of gaping press and public.

"This is an inquiry," he said, "into the death of a woman unknown, aged about thirty-five years, found dead at Binford Park Reservoir, the property of the Metropolitan Water Board. I understand that the circumstances in which she was found may give rise to further proceedings in another court and I shall accordingly order that this inquest stand adjourned for fifteen days – that is, until November 23rd."

"Twenty-third's a Friday," said the coroner's officer.

"Very well then, until November 27th. You won't mind a few more days, Inspector."

"I'm much obliged," said Inspector Gover.

In the lobby of the court, Petrella found an opportunity of passing on Luard's message.

"King of Nowhere," said Gover. "Yes. I remember it, when I was in S. Nice little place. On the canal. I heard it'd changed hands, and gone down a bit lately."

"If Howton & Co. are using it as a hideout," said Petrella, "it must have sunk without a trace. Shall I come with you?"

"I expect I can manage," said Gover. "Don't want to frighten them. By the way, we've got a report from the laboratory on the clothes. I'd like you to check that against the retail list. If we get some idea where she did her shopping it might help."

By nine o'clock that evening Petrella had had enough of retail lists.

"I believe," he said to Gwilliam, "that she did it on purpose."

Sergeant Gwilliam grunted. He was sitting with his own chair tilted back and his feet on the radiator and was reading the sports reports in the evening paper.

"As far as her clothes went, she seems deliberately to have chosen things that you can buy at any shop in London."

"They're saying now the Harlequins are the finest team in London. I don't believe they'd look at the old London Welsh."

"Her clothes are either all new or she washed them herself. Anyway there are no laundry marks or cleaners' tabs. Even her shoes, Smithsons Super-wear! Do you know how many shops sell them? Sixty-four in the West Central district alone."

"I remember," said Gwilliam, "one Boxing Day match against the Harlequins. I had a very terrible hangover – "

The telephone clattered. Gwilliam picked it up. Started to speak. Then slammed it down, and said, "Trouble, now."

"Where?" said Petrella. They were already moving.

"At a pub in Camden Town. Parrock Street."

"The King of Nowhere?"

"That's right," said Gwilliam.

Detective Constable Cobley had appeared from the charge room.

"We'll take the car nearest the entrance," said Gwilliam. "Pile in all of you. I'll drive."

"That's where Gover's gone, didn't you know?"

"Keep your hand on the siren," said Gwilliam. "You all right, Tom?"

"Fine," said Cobley. His huge body was wedged in the back of the police tender, which was already rocking as Gwilliam steadily gathered speed.

They passed the Old Mother Red Cap, at the corner of Camden High Street, took an optimistic view of the traffic lights, and beat it for fifty yards along the main road, then right, and right again into Parrock Street.

The symptoms of trouble were evident. A few men outside a door and an apprehensive crowd, mostly boys and women, on the pavement opposite.

A desultory free-for-all seemed to be going on inside, and through the steamed-up glass of the front window Petrella thought he could see the blue of a police uniform.

"There's a back entrance," he said, "by the canal. The turning at the end of the street. I'll go round."

"All right," said Gwilliam. He put his shoulder to the front door and pushed it open. Petrella had time to see this, then he was running, Cobley with him.

"Down here," he said.

It was a narrow alley, ending in high gates, with some sign painted on them. Cobley made a back, hoisted Petrella up, and was pulled up in turn. They dropped into a littered yard.

"The canal bank's through here somewhere," said Petrella. He wished he had brought his torch.

41

"Look out you don't fall in then," said Cobley. He was less excited than Petrella. They felt their way along the narrow cinder path. "It's the sixth house along. I counted."

Suddenly they were aware that figures were moving, in the dark, ahead of them, but away from them.

Things happened then, in no sort of order. Petrella jumped forward, felt an opponent, and grabbed him. As he grabbed, he slipped, and they came down together in a heap. Someone then stepped on both of them. Cobley, by the weight of him.

There was a pounding of footsteps ahead and a muffled roar as action was joined farther up the bank. Then the toe of a boot caught Petrella squarely in the middle of the forehead and the next thing he knew was that he was on his hands and knees, in the darkness, being sick.

As the nausea passed, he felt hands under his arms lifting him up.

"Are you all right, Sergeant?"

"What's happened?" said Petrella. He found that he could just stand.

"Two of 'em," said Cobley. "One of 'em knocked you cold. I pitched the other one into the canal. Just to see if he could swim."

"I'm all right now," said Petrella. The world around him was steadying, and if he concentrated he could focus. "Did he?" he added.

"Did he what?"

"Swim."

"I'm afraid so. I heard someone get out the other side. Your man scarpered too."

"We'd better go in now," said Petrella. The particular stable door they had come to lock seemed to have been kicked in their faces, but they might as well finish the job.

Cobley found the gate and pushed it open. They were in a dark, stone-paved enclosure, which smelt of beer. Ahead of them was more darkness, lit by a dim internal light. A long way away a loud argument was going on, and Petrella recognized Gwilliam's voice.

"The back door's open, Sergeant," said Cobley softly. He touched it with his foot and it swung wide. They could see the shadowy outlines of a room, lit by a dying coal fire.

"Try the light," said Petrella.

There came a booming from the middle distance.

"I don't care whether it's a private room or not." It was Gwilliam's voice. "Will you open that door or do I kick it down?"

"It's all right, Dai," shouted Petrella. "Don't wreck the place. It's too late. They've gone."

Then two things happened. Cobley, on their side, found the room switch and turned on the light. From the other side, Sergeant Gwilliam put his broad foot to the door and kicked the lock out. The door burst inwards, narrowly missing Petrella.

In the light they saw a shabby parlour, in disorder, furniture overturned and glass broken; and Detective Inspector Gover lying in the middle of the worn carpet, his head at an awkward angle, pillowed on a damp, dark patch of his own still-running blood.

5

Kellaway

"I don't see any alternative," said Barstow. "Heaven knows, it isn't a thing I like doing, going outside the division and the district, but if they leave me short of my proper establishment, and send one of my only two available divisional inspectors to America on exchange – and what he's going to learn there, you tell me – and the other goes and gets himself kicked on the head, like a rookie – "

"Perhaps I could – " said Haxtell.

"Certainly not. You're nearly past the post with Corinne Hart. It'd be stupid to put someone else on to that now." He paused, and glared round as if waiting for contradiction. When none came he said, "How is Gover?"

"I looked in at the hospital this morning," said Petrella. "He's still unconscious."

He himself had a big blue bruise in the middle of his forehead, and the corner of his right eye was held together by a strip of sticking plaster.

"You don't look more than two parts conscious yourself," said Barstow amiably. He stared at the blotting paper in front of him. It was a difficult decision.

"I'm going to ask Central to let us have someone to take on the reservoir case, until you're free," he said to Haxtell. "It's turned into a gang matter now. If Howton and his friends are mixed up in it – and it looks as if they are – it's as much the concern of S and D as it is of this division, so it won't do any harm having someone from headquarters to co-ordinate it." But he was arguing with himself, and the others knew it. For the head of one of the London districts to call in a detective super-intendent from the Central pool at Scotland Yard is quite rare enough to be remarkable, and remarked upon.

"It shouldn't be for long," said Haxtell. "I'm nearly through."

Barstow turned on Petrella. "Until they send someone else, you're in charge. Don't lose your head. There's plenty of routine stuff to do. We won't keep you."

Petrella removed himself. It was true that there was plenty to do, and he stood for a moment turning over in his mind just what it was he ought to do next. The reservoir could wait. If there were any clues there, they would keep for a bit longer. At the moment it was people, not things, that mattered.

He told the duty sergeant where he was going and set out. The cold bright autumn weather was a tonic. It was impossible to stay depressed whilst feet rang on the hard bright pavement and the blood stirred under the lash of the north wind.

Corum Street lies on the Chalk Farm side of Camden Town, in an area which had been slipping downhill for a hundred years with the stealthy inevitability of a glacier.

He climbed the crumbling front steps of No. 39, stepped past a battery of empty milk bottles, and studied the row of cards and bells. He decided that "Flat D. Mrs Jean Fraser. Three rings" was the one he wanted. He rang three times and waited. Nothing happened for a long time.

He pushed on the front door, which opened, revealing a strip of linoleum and a marble reproduction of the Winged Victory of Samothrace covered with a bee veil. The hallway was clean enough, and there was a faint smell of floor polish; but there was a much stronger smell of people; of too many people, living together, in too little space.

Flat D was on the third floor. Petrella rang three more times and knocked three times, and breathed in three times and out three times, but Flat D remained unresponsive. He was on the point of retiring when the door opposite opened and an old man came out. He had white hair, a white moustache, and a look of forgotten campaigns.

"You're wanting Jean?" he said.

"Yes," said Petrella. "Mrs Fraser."

"She's out all day. At work, you know."

"It's rather important," said Petrella. "I wonder – do you happen to know where she works?"

The old man shook his head. He thought it was something to do with toffee. His mind was clearly on the Diamond Jubilee of Queen Victoria.

"She's generally back by half past seven," he said.

Petrella thanked him and withdrew. He spent the rest of the morning in an endeavour, which he knew to be fruitless when he started on it, but which had to be carried through, to identify certain unidentifiable articles of clothing and footwear.

It was early afternoon when he got back to Crown Road, and the first thing that caught his eye was a deep, fresh scratch on the linoleum in the passage, which seemed to indicate that some heavy furniture had been moved. Then he saw a white card pinned to the door of the interview room and he read, in neat print:

D/SUPT. C O KELLAWAY
D/SERGT. ALBERT DODDS

The reinforcements had arrived.

"They're doing us proud," said Petrella to Gwilliam.

"We'll be in the headlines all right now," said Gwilliam.

There are, and there always will be, certain detective officers whom the public takes to its heart. They are usually members of the Investigations Department at Scotland Yard which the newspapers style the Murder Squad, although its work is by no means confined to murders. Their appearance, and reappearance, in the press as they speed to the help of the provincial forces ensures them a steady flow of publicity; a matter which some of them deplore more than others. "Cris" Kellaway, as he was known to a million readers of the Daily and Sunday press, deplored it not at all. A big, handsome, black-haired, strong-chinned man, he would have made an excellent rear admiral of the blue-water school. He was popularly supposed to have, in manuscript form, no less than three volumes of his memoirs already written and only awaiting his departure from the Force to be released for publication.

"He's a great man for bull," said Petrella. "But he seems to get results."

"Quite a change from gentle Gover," agreed Gwilliam. "You'd better go and say hello. He wants to see you."

When Petrella went in, Kellaway was alone, but his presence filled the tiny room. He got up, squeezed out from behind his desk, shook hands with Petrella, and took a stand in front of the empty fireplace.

"I'm glad to have you working with me," he said. "I did a job with Luard the other day and he told me about you. He said you were the only man in the CID who could tell the difference between claret and burgundy without looking at the label on the bottle."

"Luard and I were at recruit school together," said Petrella. "You've got to make allowances for that."

"I never make allowances," said Kellaway, "for myself or anyone else. That's why I'm so damned unpopular." He grinned, showing teeth as big and as white as Red Riding Hood's grand-mother's. "Now about this case. I'll tell you what I think – that way we shall all start by thinking the same."

Petrella could only recall, afterwards, that such was the impact of Kellaway's personality that at the time this sounded like sense. What Kellaway thought, his subordinates would *naturally* think too.

"This is a gang killing. Howton and his friends. The Camden Town mob, or whatever fancy name they're using now. They're all the same, these mobs. First they throw their weight about with people who are scared of them, and they get away with it. And that makes them feel good. Then they go a bit further, and perhaps they get away with that. Now they've used their feet on a police officer, which means they're asking for trouble. If Charlie Gover dies, they know just what's coming to them. And I'm here to see they get it, good and hot and strong."

Petrella was on the point of asking what the connection was between the assault on Gover and the death of Rosa Ritchie, but it occurred to him, in time, that would be taken as impertinence. And he had no desire at all to be impertinent. He found Kellaway as exhilarating as rough wine drunk in the heat of the day.

"I'm going to split this business into two parts," he went on. "You and Dodds – you know Albert?"

"Yes, I know Dodds."

"I'm sure you'll get on well together – you're to tackle it from the reservoir end. Go through the whole place, take it to pieces. Question everyone in sight. I needn't tell you. Meanwhile I'm going to work at the other end – I'm going after Howton. If we both do our jobs properly, then sooner or later" – the superintendent laid his strong, white hands on the desk in front of him, index fingers extended – "the ends will meet." As the tips of the fingers came closer Petrella would not have been in the least surprised to see a spark jump across the gap.

He said, rather breathlessly, "Right, sir. That's quite clear. I'll be getting on with it. As a matter of fact, I'd arranged to have a word with the woman Rosa shared rooms with. She's a Scots woman called Jean Fraser."

"I won't stand in your way," said Kellaway genially. "Watch out, though. I know these Scots girls – "

Petrella found Sergeant Dodds on the bank of the reservoir, a squat, swarthy, cheerful character with a look of the Foreign Legion about him. He knew him as a top-ranking darts player, three times London champion, and on one notable occasion runner-up in the *News of the World* National Finals, at the Albert Hall, where he was beaten in two straight legs by that legendary Midlander, Joey Carmichael.

"What cheer, Pat," he said. "Come and tell me where I start."

Petrella grinned. It was a feeling he had already experienced himself. Where, if at all, in those miles of shrubbery, those acres of placid water, lay any clue to the seven-week-old killing of Rosa Ritchie?

"I suppose we ought to drag the reservoir," he said.

"Have you ever done it?" said Dodds. "I dragged a canal once, near Woking. It took a week to do the job properly. Now, if you took the total area of that canal and divided it into this reservoir, it'd go about a hundred times, which means that this time next year we'd have just about worked up to the halfway line."

"I don't think it's much good crawling round all those bushes on the bank."

Dodds shuddered.

"On the other hand," went on Petrella, "it occurred to me that it might be worth starting by looking for the boat."

"What boat?"

"The one that belongs in the boathouse, down there, at the bottom of the cottage garden."

They went down to have a look.

"There could have been a boat there," agreed Dodds. "Not to say there's anything fishy about it being missing. The Water Board might have moved it."

"Let's have a word with the foreman."

Dodds said, "Yes, let's." It was quite clear that any activity was welcome which postponed the moment when he might have to start crawling through a quarter of a mile of wet, tangled, and steeply sloping shrubbery.

The foreman agreed that it was a funny thing about the boat. He had thought so before, but it hadn't been his place to speak, the boat not being in his charge. And anyway, when Ricketts' successor came along the matter would probably be cleared up.

"Ricketts?"

"Intake attendant," said Petrella. "Lived in that cottage until quite recently. Got fed up and walked out on them."

"He couldn't take the boat with him, hardly," said the foreman. "If it was there before, it'll be about somewhere."

"How often," said Dodds, "do you have occasion to search through this little lot?" He indicated the shrubbery.

"Nothing to do with me," said the foreman. "My job's to keep the cut clear. I believe they have it thinned out about once every two years."

"And that's the sort of service we pay our water rates for," said Dodds. "Come on, Patrick. You go one way and I'll go the other, and we'll meet at the far end – if we're still alive."

It was Petrella who found the boat. He had reached a point on the west bank, towards the northern tip of the reservoir, immediately under a path which led up to a high, stockaded fence. Behind the fence, he guessed, must lie the railway workshops; and beyond them again, the main line.

What he actually saw was a short piece of rusty chain, wound twice round a stake, at the water's edge. The other end seemed, at first sight, to be made fast under water, but when he bent his back and pulled there was a faint stirring of free movement.

He shouted to Dodds and between them they hauled from the water, and halfway up on to the concrete apron, the remains of an old pram dinghy.

"Stove in," said Dodds. "Stove in and left to rot." There were two big holes in the bottom. "Probably did it with the butt of an oar. I don't suppose those are far away either."

The prospect of something concrete to look for seemed to have revived his spirits. In ten minutes they had retrieved from the bushes behind the path two oars, three duckboards, a footrest, and two cork fenders.

"Signs of thought here," said Dodds. He surveyed the salvage. "Someone takes this boat from the boat shed. Rows across to the north end of the reservoir and sinks the boat. But first he takes out anything that might float and give him away. Right?"

"Right."

"Then he goes up this path – turns right at the top, because it's the only way he perishing well can turn – and what next?"

"He climbs the fence. One foot on that tree stump, another on that bolt head, like so. A bit of a pull – and he's up."

Petrella straddled the fence, puffing slightly.

"Tarzan of the North London Water Board," said Dodds, approving. "What's on the other side?"

"It's a yard," said Petrella. "And a lot of workshops, and a light railway line and – yes – a gate out to the road."

"That's it, then. That's the way he went."

"Quite a few people about."

"Not at night."

"Not so easy at night. Unless he'd worked it all out before-hand."

"Of course he'd worked it out beforehand," said Dodds. "This is a murderer we're talking about. A careful chap."

Petrella returned to earth, and dusted himself down. "The only thing I don't see," he said, "is why he should do it at all. Why didn't he go out of the main gate. At that time of night, it'd be safe enough. A lot safer than all this caper."

"Don't run before you can walk," said Dodds. "Everything will be clear as daylight before we've finished. Talking of which, we can't do much more this evening. I spotted a nice little pub on the way in. Got a dartboard too. Let's go and earn ourselves a pint."

"Not more than one, then," said Petrella weakly. "I've got a date with a girl."

When he got to Corum Street, he found that life had ebbed back into its derelict creeks and backwaters. Most of the windows had lights in them, and there were two empty prams in the hall.

When he knocked on the door of Flat D, a voice said, "Come along in, whoever you are."

Petrella pushed the door open and looked inside. There was no front hall. Flat D proved to be two intercommunicating rooms. The nearest of them was a living-room, with one of those contraptions which becomes a bed at the whisk of your hostess' hand: the farther one, as far as he could see through the open door, was a bedroom, which, no doubt, could equally easily become a sitting-room.

Standing in the communicating doorway was a fluffy-haired, brown-eyed, comfortable-looking woman of thirty – thirty-five – forty? Petrella's bachelor mind boggled at the problem.

"Do I know you," she said, "or have you come to the wrong flat?" It was a Lowland voice, but it had an inner core of toughness, an acquired metropolitan hardness.

"Mrs Fraser?"

"That's me."

"I'm Detective Sergeant Petrella."

"Oh, yes."

"I expect you're surprised."

"Not a bit. Is this going to take long enough for me to ask you to sit down?"

"I – well – I don't know."

"Sit down, then," said the lady, relenting a little.

"You said you weren't surprised," said Petrella, settling cautiously into a wicker chair. "Why was that? Most people *are* surprised when – "

"The colonel – he lives opposite – told me you'd been asking for me this morning. He said 'from his face you'd call him a schoolboy, but from his boots he's a policeman.' "

"And I thought his mind was miles away."

"Don't let him fool you. That's how he makes his living. You didn't come to talk about him?"

"No," said Petrella. "I came to talk about Mrs Ritchie. You shared these rooms, didn't you?"

'They're my rooms. She had the use of one of them for a while."

"Could you tell me about that? When she left, and so on."

Jean looked at him speculatively, and Petrella got the impression that she was quite used to dealing with policemen; but policemen, perhaps, of a different sort. Not ones who said "Could you" and "Would you".

"If you like," she said. "Though it's all ancient history now. She came here in – when would it be – January or February of this year. Some time about then. She left toward the end of September."

"Do you remember which day?"

"How should I remember that?"

"Were you surprised when she left?"

"No more surprised than when she came. If you're a policeman you'll know that her husband was a criminal."

"Yes. I knew that."

"Well, I can read, Mr – "

"Petrella."

"That sounds foreign."

"It's Spanish, actually."

"Uh, huh. I was saying, I can read. When I saw in the papers that Monk Ritchie was out of prison – and later that he was believed to have escaped abroad – I formed my own conclusions."

"Yes," said Petrella. "I thought that was the way of it. What time of day did she go?"

"I couldn't be certain. I left her here when I went to work in the morning. She was gone when I came back."

"Without taking any of her things with her?"

"That's true. But she hadn't a lot, poor soul."

"Are her things still in the room?"

"Am I a millionairess? It's been let twice since then. There's a Polish lady has it now. Would you like to see it? Madame Jablonski is out. She works in a café. She won't object, I dare say."

"How many times would you say the room has been cleaned since Mrs Ritchie left it?"

"Every day. And repainted and papered last month. Madame did it herself. She's very artistic."

"Then I don't think," said Petrella, "that there's a great deal of point in my looking at it. What became of Rosa's things?"

"I packed them in a bag and put them in the storeroom down-stairs. Do you want to see them?"

"I'm not sure," said Petrella. "I may do. First, could you tell me – " He was unwrapping the parcel he had brought with him. Mrs Fraser seemed to sense something either from his tone of voice or from his movements, and she was suddenly still.

"Do you recognize this dress? Or any of these clothes? Or the shoes?"

In the silence he heard a door open on the top landing and the voices of people speaking on the stairs.

"Where did you get them?"

"I'll tell you in a moment," said Petrella. "First, if you don't mind – are they Mrs Ritchie's?"

"Yes." She had scarcely looked at them. "They're hers. In fact, two of them – that and that – are mine. I lent them to her. Where did you find them?"

"We found a woman," said Petrella, "on the bank of one of the reservoirs. You might have seen it in the papers – but it didn't make much of a splash."

"And that was Rosa?"

"From what you tell me, there seems no doubt about it at all."

"And how – what had happened? Can you tell me that?"

"She had been shot. That's in the papers now."

"By her husband?"

"We don't know that."

"It would be her husband. Who else?"

"We may have to ask you to identify the body formally. Unless we can find a relative. Would you do that?"

"She'd no relatives down here that I know of. She came from Ayrshire. It's where I'm from myself, that's how we came to be friends. Yes, I'll identify her, if I have to – "

"We may be able to do it some other way."

"I'll give you the name of the place I'm working." She scribbled on a piece of paper. "It's a place that makes sweets. Don't come after me there. I've a reputation to lose."

Petrella promised. Out in the street, it had started to rain again. He turned up the collar of his coat against it and stumped off. He was thinking about Mrs Fraser, and how nice she was, and how poor. And that she had become neither hysterical nor self-important about the violent death of her friend. He was thinking too deeply to have an eye out for his surroundings, and he missed a quick movement. Behind him, a man had detached himself from the shadows and moved cautiously out. Slowly though he moved, the dip and roll of his progress was unmistakable. Boot Howton looked first to right and left, then climbed the steps of No. 39 and disappeared into the hall.

6

The Outgoing of an
Intake Attendant

Petrella was down at the reservoir by half past eight next morning. It was a calm, bright, cold winter's day, a day of nipped fingers and steaming breath. He found Sergeant Dodds already at work.

A lorry and trailer stood in the open space in front of the cottage and Dodds and three men were offloading a flat-bottomed boat. It looked like an infantry-assault craft.

"Now you have got out of bed," said Dodds, "you can come and lend a hand. I'm warning you it's a lot heavier than it looks."

Between them they staggered onto the landing stage, lowered one side, lifted the other, and heaved. The boat hit the surface with a solid ker-splash, sending a long ripple out over the surface of the water and fetching a protest from a sleepy swan.

"She floats," said Dodds. "What next, George?"

"The detector gear has to be fixed in," said the young man who seemed to be in charge of the party. "We can handle that now. Just tell us the line you want to take."

"You're to cover a strip," said Dodds, "ten or twelve feet wide. Say two yards either side of the boat. Go straight across from this landing stage to the far end. There's a point you can lay on. It isn't easy to see from here. Where a path goes up through the bushes."

"I'll walk round in a minute and stick a flag in," said the young man. "You show me just where you want it. It's going to take me a bit of time to rig the gear. I'll tell you when we're ready."

He went into a huddle with his two mechanics, and Petrella heard snatches of conversation about something which sounded like "the fixer magnet". Then all three men went back to the lorry and started rolling back the tarpaulin.

"What's it all about?"

"Just a bit of Chris Kellaway's famous drive and efficiency," said Dodds. "This is an up-to-date salvage unit. Private firm. George, here, does the frog stuff, when it's called for. The other two operate the box of tricks. It's a detector. Something the navy dreamed up for dealing with limpet mines. You can drag an electrical gadget across the bottom and if it comes within smelling distance of any metal it goes 'ping'. In fact, it goes several different sorts of 'ping' and the bright boy sitting in the boat can tell how much metal, and what sort, and how far off, and so on."

"And then the frogman goes down and has a look at it?"

"Right. And rather him than me this weather."

"I don't know," said Petrella. "You can wear warm clothes inside the suit. As a matter of fact, I've always wanted – "

"Not today," said Dodds. "Have a heart. You get it out of your system some other time. This is strictly a professional job."

One of the men in the boat looked up from screwing an instrument panel to the cross-thwart of the boat and said, "How deep's the water?"

Dodds consulted his plan. "Twenty feet in the middle," he said. "Six feet at the sides. Gravel bottom, shelving gently. Piece of cake."

The man grunted, picked up a ratchet screwdriver, and screwed in a screw as if he hated it.

"You've got to hand it to Chris," said Dodds. "He does get ideas – sometimes. You take an ordinary piece of water, a pond or a river or a canal. You put a sensitive bit of machinery like this over it, and what happens? 'Ping' – and up comes an old kettle. 'Ping-ping' and it's a washtub with a hole in it. 'Ping-ping-ping' and it's an – "

"I get your point," said Petrella.

"Here you've got a nice clear bottom. Shouldn't be *anything* there except water. So every time she sounds off, it's worth going down to have a look."

"And you're starting on this particular line because you think that whoever it was took the boat rowed her straight across and may have dropped – something or other – overboard. What *are* we hoping to find?"

"Like all good policemen," said Dodds, "we're keeping strictly open minds."

The frogman now appeared, carrying a red-and-white survey flag on a stick, and he and Dodds wandered off together to mark the aiming point.

Petrella looked at his watch and remembered that the reason he was there was that he had a date with Mr Lundgren at nine o'clock.

Punctual to the minute, a smart little car drew up on the gravel sweep and the resident supply engineer jumped out.

"Good morning, Sergeant," he said. "How are things progressing – what on earth's going on?"

"It's a treasure hunt – modern style," said Petrella, and explained.

"I hope they don't disturb a pair of little crested grebes," said Lundgren. "This is the first year they've wintered here. Their nest's over there, near where those two men are standing. What the devil are they waving that flag for?"

Petrella explained this too.

"Let's stick flags up all round and have a regatta. Why not!" said Mr Lundgren sourly, and Petrella registered the thought that if Superintendent Kellaway had been just that little bit more tactful he would have told the supply engineer what he planned to do and got him on his side first.

"Do you mean to say," went on Lundgren, "that you're working on the assumption that the murderer shot this woman – she *was* shot, wasn't she? – I thought it said so in the papers – and then took the boat, and rowed it across, and sunk it, and went up the path and climbed over a ten-foot fence. Why didn't he walk out of the front gate? It's locked, but it isn't all that difficult to climb over. I've done it myself before now, and I'm no gymnast."

This was precisely the point that was worrying Petrella, so instead of answering the question he asked one himself. "In fact," he said, "had you noticed that the boat was missing?"

"No," said Lundgren. He sounded a bit upset about this. "I expect we should have spotted it when we made a proper check. That would be when the next man came in."

"And the house."

"We'll look at that now. I brought the keys with me."

"Are we the first people to go in since Ricketts left?"

"Bless you, no. We may be a bit unbusinesslike, but we're not as bad as that. One of our property managers went over it as soon as we heard Ricketts had gone. Turned off the gas and electricity, and checked that Ricketts hadn't walked off with any of the Board's property."

"And had he?"

"On the contrary – now which of these two is the front-door key? – I seem to remember that he'd left quite a lot of his own stuff behind. We had it inventoried and stored away – "

(Petrella thought, Where did I hear that before? Of course, Rosa's friend Jean. "I packed them in a bag and put them in the storeroom downstairs." Two lots of belongings, waiting for two people to come back and claim them.)

"What sort of things?" he said.

"Bed linen and curtains and things like that. All these doors are apt to stick. Give it a push."

Cold and dark and silent, the house awaited them, an old woman, her hands folded, expectant of indignities.

"Smells damp to me," said Mr Lundgren. "We'll have to get it thoroughly aired before the next man comes in. I'll go and open the shutters. Then we shall have a bit more light."

One door on the right of the tiny hallway opened into the living-room; another, at the end, into the kitchen. The stairs rose straight out of the hall.

"It's a simple sort of but and ben," said Lundgren, "but it's handy. There's a nice bedroom, and a modern bathroom and lavatory upstairs. Main drainage, of course. And electricity, only it's turned off just now."

"I expect it's very nice," said Petrella, repressing a shudder. "When it's warm and cheerful. Just at the moment – "

"I'll open the shutters."

They gazed round the living-room. The carpet had been rolled up and the floor scrubbed. An imitation-leather sofa and two armchairs were stacked together in front of the unprotected grate. Petrella ran a finger along the top of the nearest chair, producing a faint powdering of greeny white mould. Lundgren was right. The place was damp.

"We had it cleaned right out. I expect we shall redecorate before the next man comes in."

"Yes," said Petrella. "What I'd like to do is have a word with the man who saw it first. Did he get the impression that Ricketts had taken his time about going? Had he packed all his things up carefully? That'd take time, you see. Or did he just cram what he wanted into a suitcase and push off?"

"I'm not sure," said Lundgren. "There was something in the report – I've got it at the office. I'll look at it when I get back. No, I remember. It was the washing. The laundry had delivered a week's washing. It was still in the porch when our man came round."

"There's nothing in that," said Petrella. "Anyone might forget their washing. Let's look upstairs."

The bedroom was furnished simply with a bed, now stripped to its springs, a chest of drawers and cupboard. The chest and cupboard were empty and clean.

"Some of the things left in here would certainly have been his," said Lundgren. "The sheets and pillowcases, for instance. The blankets and bedding were supplied by us. That vase now – I'm not sure – "

"Even if I'd had plenty of time," said Petrella, "I think I might have managed to leave that behind." The vase was pink, and embossed with tiny green oyster shells which formed the words "A present from Whitstable."

"Not absolutely my taste," agreed Lundgren. "But some people like that sort of thing. Here's the bathroom." This, too, was bare, except for a cork bath mat and several dozen rusty razor blades, which had been overlooked on top of the medicine cupboard.

"Well, he took his toothbrush," said Lundgren.

"And his towel. Let's try the kitchen."

Here there was more to be seen. The room had been scrubbed and tidied, but they found a cupboard full of tins and packets – corn flour, tea, sugar (turned by the damp into a granular lump), and other accessories of the kitchen. In the larder stood a plate with a remnant on it that defied immediate analysis. There was a crusted saucepan pushed away on a shelf over the gas stove, and beside it a dry kettle.

"It'd be interesting, too, to know if he left any washing up behind him. That'd be a pointer to the time of day he left. Perhaps your man could tell us that? And by the way – I don't think I ever asked you. What day did he go?"

"Now, that I can tell you exactly," said Lundgren. "I found the copy of his telegram on my desk when I got to my office that Monday. It had been sent off two days before, on Saturday night."

Petrella swallowed hard.

"Saturday?"

"That's right. Saturday, September 22nd. I was due to start my holiday on the following Friday – that's how I know."

The world, which had been rotating comfortably on its axis, stood still; then started again with a lurch. Petrella said softly, "What a fool! What a fool! What a brainless, clueless fool!"

Lundgren gaped at him.

"Myself, I mean. Fool not to ask such an obvious question right at the start."

"Is the date important?"

"Certainly it's important. In fact, right now it's the most important thing in the case. We've got to get hold of Ricketts, and get hold of him quick. Do you know where he is?"

"Well," said Mr Lundgren. "No. Really, I'm afraid I don't. We never made any real effort to trace him. We were sorry he left us, but he wasn't a criminal or anything. Why is it suddenly so important to know where he is?"

From outside, on the reservoir, there came a shout. One of the men in the boat was on his feet and calling to the bank. Then the excitement seemed to subside. The man sat down again.

In this space of time, Petrella had come to an important conclusion. He wanted Lundgren's help. And he would only get it at the cost of telling him the truth or a good deal of it. And this he did.

When he had finished, Lundgren said, "I must say, it sounds pretty conclusive to me. The woman was Rosa Ritchie, you say?"

"Almost certainly, yes. The dental check should be conclusive. But I think we might assume it."

"And she was killed on Saturday, September 22nd. Most probably in the afternoon or evening, wouldn't you think? The other men go off duty at one o'clock on a Saturday. Except for Ricketts."

"Exactly," said Petrella. "*Except for Ricketts*. And your evidence shows that he cleared out that same evening. Do you happen to remember exactly what time his telegram to you was sent off?"

"I don't remember," said Lundgren. "But I've got the confirmation copy in my files. Would you like to see it? I can run you back to my office in the car."

"Grand. I'll have to telephone my superintendent. We'll arrange to have the place gone over thoroughly. And I'll need help for that. Not that we're likely to find much now."

"You don't think, do you," said Lundgren, as they got into the car, "that Ricketts – "

"Shot Mrs Ritchie?"

"Yes."

"It's not impossible. It doesn't quite fit in with one or two other things. I think this is the sort of case where it's a mistake to jump to conclusions."

He caught Kellaway at his desk and told him what had happened. After he had finished speaking, there was a very slight pause. It was as if the superintendent was trying to fit the news into an existing pattern of notions, and the rough edges would not quite match. Then he said, "Yes, of course. That's a vital piece of news. I'll have a team sent down right away to go over that cottage with a tooth-comb. Keep on at the Ricketts angle and let me know what happens."

In Lundgren's office, a little research produced the telegram.

"That's our private stamp," said Lundgren. "It shows that it was dealt with here on the morning of September 24th. Otherwise it's exactly as it was received. Dispatched from Leicester Square Head Post Office, you see, at 9:45 p.m."

The telegram was addressed "Metropolitan Water Board North West Area" and said, "Am leaving job and cottage tonight going Blackpool Regret inconvenience Writing Ricketts."

"Terse, and to the point," said Petrella.

"It was a considerable shock," said Lundgren. "When a man pulls out suddenly like that, you can't help wondering if everything's in order in his department. Not that Ricketts handled any of our money."

"Everything at the cottage was in order. And his gear?"

"Unless he was responsible for the boat, there weren't any deficiencies at all. As a matter of fact, we were in pocket by two weeks' pay. For some reason he hadn't drawn that Friday or the Friday before."

"Sounds like a capitalist."

"It's odd you should say that," said Lundgren. "He didn't make any sort of show, but I had the impression that he wasn't broke by any means, I can't remember why I thought it. Maybe because he always dressed well off duty."

"I take it he *didn't* write from Blackpool."

"Not a word."

Petrella said, "I seem to remember you telling me that you were in the army with Ricketts."

"That's right. He was in my battery during the war. We used him in the Battery Office, for clerical duties. He was as fit as a fiddle, but a bit over age for work on the guns."

"Tell me all that you can remember about him."

Lundgren considered.

"I remember him best," he said, "in the very first months of the war. We were all new to our jobs and feeling our way as we went. That was when the old soldier came into his own. Ricketts was just that – an old soldier *par excellence.*"

"A regular?"

"No. I don't think so. I mean that he'd seen service in the First World War, and active service at that. He wore the ribbon of the MM. I believe he lied about his age to get to the front."

Petrella made a calculation. "If he was seventeen or thereabouts in the last year of the war, he'd be in his late fifties now."

"That's about right. He was in his early forties when this war started. An active, vigorous, handsome man. Hair going a bit grey, but that somehow gave him an extra touch of dependability. And he certainly knew how to get things done. He was an extra right hand to an inexperienced subaltern like me. You know the sort of man."

"Yes," said Petrella. "You've described him very well. The only thing is – don't take this the wrong way – he seems a bit too good for the job he landed up in."

"I had just the same thought myself," said Lundgren. "You know what a difference uniform makes to a man. I'd got used to seeing him slopping round in battledress. When he called on me here, in answer to our advertisement, my first reaction was surprise that he should have been applying for the job at all. He was neatly dressed. His hair a bit greyer and he'd taken to glasses, and altogether he looked just the sort of person who comes up to town on the 8:30 in a first-class carriage, as likely as not. I assumed he was hard up, and left it at that."

"Did he say anything about it? Why he wanted the job – and so on – ?"

"Not a word. I gather one of the attractions was the cottage. He said he liked privacy."

"And that was – how long ago?"

"Two years, almost to the day. He started work in early September. And I patted myself on the back that the Board had made a good bargain."

"No complaints?"

"None at all. It wasn't very exacting work. But he did it excellently."

Petrella picked up the telegram and read it through again.

"And you never took any steps to trace him?"

"We had no reason to. As I said, his account was in credit – more than enough to pay for the cleaning of the cottage and make good any little deficiencies."

"And at the time you had no doubt that this telegram came from Ricketts."

Lundgren looked up quickly.

"I haven't any doubt about it now," he said. "What are you getting at?"

"Didn't it strike you as odd that the telegram shouldn't have been addressed to you personally? It must have been intended as a sort of farewell message. And it was you who got him the job. If there was anyone he was letting down it was you."

"Yes – "

"If he felt shy of addressing it to you by name – and he may have been – why not 'Resident Supply Engineer' with the proper address of your office? I suppose he knew it? Just to put 'Metropolitan Water Board, North West Area' – isn't that a bit risky? It might have landed up in anyone's in-tray."

"It never occurred to me," said Lundgren slowly. "In fact, you see, this is the headquarters of the North West Area, and I'm in charge, so it naturally came to me. What's your idea about it?"

"I couldn't help noticing that there's a board up outside the reservoir with exactly those words on it. 'Metropolitan Water Board. North West Area.' It occurred to me that if someone who didn't know much about your set-up wanted to send a telegram as if it came from Ricketts, that's just how he'd address it."

There was a long silence while Lundgren stared at Petrella.

Then he said, "If that's right, where's Ricketts?"

The telephone on the desk saved Petrella the difficulty of answering. Lundgren picked it up and said, "Yes?" and listened for a moment. "Yes, he's here with me now. Hold on," and to Petrella, "It's for you."

"It can't be," said Petrella. "No one knows I'm here. Hullo."

"We've been looking for you," said the voice of Sergeant Dodds. "You're to come back to the reservoir, as quick as possible."

"What's happening? How did you know where I was?"

"The Dodds bush telegraph system. I can't tell you anything more on this line. But we've found something."

7

Kellaway Puts On His Best Hat

"There she is," said Sergeant Dodds. "Wotter beauty." A clean sheet of lining paper had been spread on the living-room table, and in the middle of the paper lay a pistol.

"Considering it's been under water all that time, it's not in bad shape at all, would you say?"

It was an automatic, of about the same size as a .45, its working parts of dull metal, its handle of some black synthetic stuff. It had, as Sergeant Dodds said, stood up well to its immersion.

"I'd guess it had been pretty well greased up, too," said Dodds. "Packed away in grease probably."

"What sort is it? I've never seen one like it."

"You've never seen one like it! That's because you're young and innocent. You'd have seen plenty of them the other side of the Channel in 1945. It's a German Army pistol."

"I thought all Germans carried Lugers."

"Only in films. This is the regular issue job. It's a good gun, too. I've used one myself. Reliable up to twenty-five yards, and anyone trying to shoot someone more than twenty-five yards away with a pistol wants their head examined. Who's this?"

There came the sound of a car door slamming and Dodds jumped across to the window.

"It's Chris. And I bet he's pleased with life. Talk about a hunch."

It was Superintendent Kellaway. He bounced into the room like the favorite coming into the ring under the bright arc lights. He was followed, more slowly, by a fat person, with a head of black curly hair and the tight smile of a man who knows what he is talking about.

"I got hold of Charlie Fenwick as soon as I heard your news," said Kellaway, "and brought him along. We'll turn the gun over to him and he'll tell us all about it."

The fat man picked up the gun carefully but firmly, like an experienced nurse handling a difficult baby.

"A *P*38," he said. "The normal army type. Too common to be much use for identification. You might get something out of the silencer though." He pointed to the bulbous extension, so welded by time and rust to the barrel that it seemed to be part of it. "I don't think the *P*38 was issued with a silencer. I'd say that one's an old Mauser silencer, been adapted. Damn dangerous things, really. I'd never fire a gun myself with one of them on. A fraction out of alignment and the whole thing goes off in your face."

As he spoke his pudgy hands were exploring the weapon, pressing and twisting. Now he gave the whole gun a sharp smack and the magazine clattered out onto the table.

"How long did you say this'd been in the water?"

"If we're right, six or seven weeks."

"Then someone took damned good care of it before it went in. Otherwise it'd be rusted solid by this time."

He picked up the magazine carefully, holding it by the edges with the tips of his thick but curiously delicate fingers.

"How many have been fired?" asked Kellaway.

"The maximum load's nine. I can count six here in the clip. Which is in quite remarkably good order, by the way. No sign of rust at all. There's probably one up the spout. It could have been fired twice or it could have been fired three times."

"Would a bullet out of one of these look like a .45 bullet?"

"They're both made of lead," said Fenwick cryptically. He was still examining the magazine, holding it under the full light of the window. Now he rubbed his fingernail very gently across the surface, and said, "You can still feel the mineral jelly it was packed in. Wonderful stuff for waterproofing. Fifty times as good as grease. All the same, I don't believe I've ever seen anything quite like that before. Not after such a long immersion. I can only suppose that the magazine was an exceptionally tight fit; perhaps it belonged originally to another gun altogether."

"What are you getting at?" said Kellaway.

"*If* it was an exceptionally tight fit, and well packed with grease to start with, you might get an airlock. See what I mean? No water would get inside the magazine sleeve at all. Not for a long time, anyway."

"So what?"

"It's not my department. Nothing to do with me at all. But wouldn't you say that was a print?"

They crowded round him.

"Can't see a thing," said Kellaway.

"Look. When I tilt her. Now."

"By God!" said Kellaway, and the invocation was so heartfelt that it sounded almost reverent. "You're right. It is a sort of print. Right on the panel of the magazine."

"What saved it," said Fenwick, "is that the moisture couldn't get at it. Wonderful example of the working of Providence. Like the pearl in the oyster. Waiting there till Doomsday for the lucky fisherman."

But Kellaway was not listening. He had stalked away, into the middle of the room, and he stood there for a minute while he contemplated the moves which now had to be made. In the times that followed, Petrella sometimes found himself looking back to that moment. Making all allowances for luck, full credit had to be given to Kellaway. Laid on a stale scent, within twenty-four hours, he had turned up what looked very like the murder weapon, ready furnished with a print of the murderer.

He turned to Dodds.

"That search party I organized. What happened to them?"

"They're working upstairs. They finished down here."

"Who's in charge?"

"Sergeant Cobbold."

"Is he the camera man?"

"That's right," said Dodds. "A real artist. He's missed his vocation. He ought to be taking snaps on the front."

"Fetch him down. Let's see if we can get a photograph of this print right away."

Sergeant Cobbold, when it was put to him, said, certainly. The electricity had been turned on. He could plug his lamp and reflector and photograph anything they wanted right away. Might as well do the other one at the same time.

"Other what?"

"Print," said Cobbold, looking surprised. "Didn't you know we found a set of prints in here? Very nice ones too."

He walked across to the window. "On the upright. The middle one, sort of embedded in the paintwork. That's why they're still there, I guess."

He directed the light of the torch that he held on to the spot and they saw, almost startling clear, the marks of four fingertips.

"What happened," said Cobbold happily, "is someone must have come in this window from the outside. That's the way the fingertips are pointing, see. The window's open, and he pulls on this upright to get himself through. Perhaps the paint isn't quite dry, or perhaps it's a very hot day, and the paint's a bit soft."

"How long would a print like that last?" said Kellaway.

"Oh, quite a long time. Six months – maybe a year."

"In that case, we'll probably find it was the man who did the painting," said Dodds.

"Don't believe it," said Kellaway. He was riding high on his luck. That day, he knew, every jackpot would drop, every outsider would come romping home. "Photograph these as well. Then we'll send both lots down to Central and see if we can get a quick identification. If they're the same man – why, then, we're going places."

An hour later Petrella was displaying the freshly dried positives to Sergeant Blinder.

"Envelope A," he said, "photograph of a single print, taken from the magazine of a *P*38 automatic pistol."

"Do you call that a photograph?" said Sergeant Blinder. "Who took it? Cobbold? You'd have thought, all the tips I've given him, he'd know how to highlight a photograph."

"The gun it came off had been under water for more than a month. You can't expect too much."

"There's nothing wrong with the print," said Sergeant Blinder. "A very nice print indeed. It's the photograph I'm complaining about. These boys will use overhead lighting. I've told them time and again that a lateral beam – "

"Here," said Petrella hastily, "we have envelope B. A set of four fingerprints of the right hand found on the paintwork of a window jamb. We think it might be off the same man."

"That I can tell you right away they're not," said Sergeant Blinder.

"How *can* you tell?"

"Different altogether."

"I'll take your word for it. If you can make us an identification – it really is rather urgent. Superintendent Kellaway – "

Sergeant Blinder sniffed.

"When did he want it?"

"Just as soon as possible."

"Not yesterday? Or the day before yesterday?"

Petrella was in no mood for defending Superintendent Kellaway.

"No," he said. "Just as quickly as you can, that's all."

He had a lot to do himself. After a quick lunch in the canteen he took himself out to Hounds Green for another word with Lundgren. This proved to be a frustrating afternoon. Lundgren was engaged, when he arrived, but his secretary thought that he would be free at any minute. Petrella sat in the waiting-room and read through *Some notes on Water Purification by the Heck-Mueller System of Disks and Meshes*. When he had finished this, and Lundgren had still failed to appear, he went out for a cup of tea. By the time he had got back, Lundgren had appeared, looked for him, and got himself tied up again with another caller. Petrella settled down to study the *Metropolitan Water Board. Annual Infall Statistics.* At five o'clock Lundgren finally came in full of apologies.

"I can find out when the cottage was painted last," he said. "My impression is that it was certainly done when Ricketts went in, but there may have been minor maintenance jobs carried out since. As for getting the fingerprints of the painters who carried out the job – I shouldn't think it'd be difficult to find them. Only they might object to having their fingerprints taken."

"We'll need yours too," said Petrella. "You've been over the house. And your cleaner's. If you give me the names, I'll have someone sent out."

"I'm trying hard not to be inquisitive," said Lundgren, "but I take it – I take it this means you've found something."

"Yes," said Petrella. "But for goodness' sake keep it under your hat."

Lundgren followed his exposition with the keenest attention.

"If they're not the same man," he said, "the one who came in the window, and the one who fired the gun, then it looks as if perhaps Ricketts didn't – "

"There are too many possibilities at the moment," said Petrella. "Like in bridge. Whatever the experts pretend, you can't really deduce what's in all four hands just from the bidding alone. You've got to wait until a trick or two's been played."

"I'm very fond of bridge myself," said Lundgren. "We must see if we can't arrange a rubber when this unhappy business is settled – "

It was after six before Petrella got back to Crown Road, guiltily conscious that he had more or less wasted the afternoon. As soon as he got into the corridor he could tell that something had happened.

Dodds shot out of the CID room, caught sight of him, and said, "There you are, Patrick. Come on, quick!" and whisked him into Haxtell's room.

The nominal owner of the room was sitting quietly in one corner, and Chief Superintendent Barstow was installed behind his desk. Kellaway was standing in front of the fire and a bulky man with crinkly grey hair, whom Petrella knew by sight as Chief Superintendent Burrell, father of the fingerprint section at Scotland Yard, was overflowing the only other chair.

"Now we *are* all here," said Barstow, looking sourly at Petrella. "I'll recapitulate. First we have evidence that this was a gang killing." Kellaway nodded. "Second, we find a gun which is believed to belong to Howton. He's got a record of violence and has been taken once with a gun on him."

"Twice – unlawful possession of firearms – 1946 in Liverpool and 1951 in London."

"Third, he was friendly with Rosa Ritchie. It's reasonable to suppose that her husband getting out of jail precipitated some sort of crisis – and there's evidence that the killing did in fact take place on the day after he got out.

"Fourth, and last, Howton has certainly been in that cottage sometime. It looks from the position of his fingerprints as if he climbed in at an open window."

"He wouldn't have any reason that we know of for being there legitimately."

Chief Superintendent Barstow considered the matter. To the professionals gathered in the room the trend of his thoughts was as evident as if he had spoken them aloud. He was not an entirely likeable character, not a glad sufferer of fools, not beloved of his subordinates, but he had, as Petrella had observed, one admirable characteristic; he was capable of making up his mind, and he made it up quickly.

"Not good enough," he said. "Very, very nearly, but not quite. If the print on the gun had been Howton's – "

Petrella looked up quickly.

" – By the way, have you identified that print yet?"

"No, sir," said Kellaway. "I expect we shall, but it's a rather faint, single print, and that's bound to take longer. Of course, it could turn out to be one of Howton's boys."

"If it turns out to be one of Howton's boys, then he's the one we ought to charge with the murder," said Barstow reasonably. "No. The evidence so far is simply that Howton was in the cottage. His fingerprints on the window prove that. We don't know *when* he was there. But it seems highly likely that it was on the night Mrs Ritchie got killed. However, that's conjecture. What we want is positive evidence, either Howton was seen near the reservoir that night or, perhaps, something to tie him up to the shooting. What about motive?"

"As you said yourself, sir, there must have been some sort of crisis." Kellaway tried to keep the irritation out of his voice. "Monk Ritchie had got out of prison the day before. He'd go straight to the boys. They'd hide him up for the first night. Next day they'd arrange for a meeting with Rosa. She was banker to the outfit. When we put Monk away, you remember, we got very little of the stuff. It now seems clear that Rosa had got it stowed away somewhere. I'd suggest that she and Howton had been quietly turning it into cash. And maybe quietly spending it on themselves."

"If that was right, Monk would have shot Howton, not his wife."

"I should have thought," said Kellaway, managing to instil just enough deference into his voice, "that the only way to find out the truth was to pull in Howton. We'll get evidence quick enough then. His friends'll all talk, once he's inside."

"No," said Barstow. "It won't do. Get something to tie him to the reservoir. Get something to tie him to the jewels. Then we'll take a chance and charge him."

Superintendent Haxtell spoke for the first time. He had been sitting so quietly on his bed in the corner that they had all forgotten he was there.

"Corinne Hart," he said, "was killed three streets away from the reservoir."

They stared at him.

"You're not suggesting," said Barstow, at last, "that there's any connection between the two cases?"

"No, sir. But in the course of that investigation we've taken statements from more than a thousand people, including every soul living in Ogilvie Street and Mearns Street – those are the streets that run to the south and southwest of the reservoir, between it and the filter beds. And, you'll remember, we didn't just ask them about the night Corinne disappeared. We went back weeks, sometimes months. We wanted to find out if any strange man had been pestering the kids in the neighborhood."

"That's a damned good idea," said Barstow. "And it'll save a lot of time. Get a man going through those reports now, to see if he can pick up anything that'll help us in this case."

When the conference broke up, Petrella had a quick word with Dodds.

"Are you sure they haven't got these prints mixed up?" he said.

"It's an idea," said Dodds, "but I'm afraid it won't wash. The four prints off the window are a set. They belong to Howton. No doubt at all. Burrell doesn't make mistakes about fingerprints. The one on the gun's a single print. They don't even know which hand. It's going to take a lot longer to get anything out of that."

"But whoever it was, it wasn't Howton. At least, that's what Blinder told me."

"Burrell says that, too."

"But it certainly belonged to the man who loaded the gun."

"It isn't always the person who loads a gun that fires it," said Dodds.

Petrella digested this in silence.

"What's Kellaway going to do now?"

"If I know our Chris, he's kicking his desk and wishing it was Barstow's bottom. Hullo, there's the bell. We'd better go and see what he wants."

Whatever may have been his private feelings, Kellaway had them well under control.

"I'd like you," he said to Petrella, "to see if you can get a line on that jewellery. You know all your local jewellers and pawnbrokers.

And I suggest you get a bit of co-operation from Luard in S. Between the two of you you might be able to turn something up. I've had Records make me some copies of Howton's photograph. Take one with you. It might help to stir people's memories."

Which brought Petrella back again to where it had all started: to the back room of Mr Robins, Pawnbroker, Jeweller and Silversmith, with its built-in safe and its mighty, brass-bound ledger. When he saw Petrella, Mr Robins groaned.

"I knew it," he said.

"You knew what?"

"That you'd be back. I suppose they told you."

"No one's told me anything," said Petrella. "What have you been up to? Receiving stolen goods?"

Mr Robins smiled faintly. "Really, it almost looks like it," he said. "After you'd gone I took a copy of that list, the one that had all the Colegrave stuff in it, and went carefully through my deposits. I've identified six different pieces, besides the clasp you were asking me about. None of them are very large – here's the list I sent to the station. I'd have thought they'd have passed it on to you."

"I've been a bit elusive these last two days," said Petrella. He cast his eye down the list. The money given by Mr Robins for the six items totalled just over a hundred pounds, which meant that they were probably worth from twice to three times as much.

"Were they all deposited by the same person?"

"That's what's so difficult. I deal with – thirty, forty people every day."

"Does this do anything to your memory?"

Petrella took out the photograph of Howton. It was a good photograph. Not one of those close-up profiles taken in a strong light which would make the Archbishop of Canterbury look like an axe murderer, but an informal snapshot of Howton stepping off the pavement, taken, Petrella guessed, with a candid camera, buttonhole attachment, and enlarged.

"Why, yes," said Mr Robins at last. "I'd say I'd seen him in here. It's not a common sort of face, is it?"

"But do you associate it with these particular pieces of jewellery?"

"All those pieces were deposited here in the last two months. I know that's right, because my book says so. And it's in the last two months that I've seen – what's his name? – "

"Howton."

" – I've seen Howton about. The last time was about a week ago, and that reminds me. Dicky!"

A thin, white-faced, gristly boy put his head round the door and said, "Wassup?"

"It was you took in the eardrops a week ago yesterday."

" 'Sright."

"Can you remember what the customer looked like?"

"Man with a limp, would it be?"

The evening suddenly seemed brighter to Petrella; a lot brighter and a lot warmer.

"Yes," he said. "It could have been a man with a limp. Was he anything like this, Dicky?"

The boy held the photograph carefully up to the light and looked at it inscrutably. Then he put it down again, and said, "Do you mind my asking my dad something?"

"Not a bit."

"Alone."

"We'll leave you here," said Mr Robins, and went out of the door, taking the boy with him.

The minutes dragged by. Then Mr Robins reappeared.

"That's all right," he said. "He identified him. The eardrops, and a lady's watch the week before. He's a sharp boy, Dicky. He doesn't make mistakes."

"What was he worried about?"

"He didn't quite know who you were or what you were after. Don't you worry, he'll make a good witness for you."

"Yes. I rather imagine he will," said Petrella slowly.

Back at Crown Road we went straight in to report to Dodds. He found the sergeant in high good humour.

"That's the stuff, boy," he said. "We're getting our feet on the ground in all directions now. Just listen to this. Here's Rebecca Gurney. She lives – I beg your pardon, resides – at 17A Ogilvie Street, occupying the ground floor, and has a bow window overlooking the gates of the reservoir, and very little to do in life except look out of it. She deposes: 'On the evening of Saturday, September 22nd, which I remember because it was my elder sister's birthday, or would have been if she had been alive, she died twenty-five years ago and never have I allowed September 22nd to go by without thinking of her, and how I remember it was a Saturday, because the reservoir gates were shut when the men go after lunch. It was about eight in the evening but still light enough to see. I saw two men get out of a car which drove off to the top of the road and turned round and waited. The men walked up the road on the opposite pavement and disappeared. An hour later, they came back. It was dark by then but they were on my pavement this time and I saw them both clearly. One of them seemed to be keeping watch. The other climbed over the gate into the reservoir.' Question, 'Why did you not report this?' Answer, 'I was alone in the house and have no telephone. I was afraid to go outside. I did not like the look of the men.' Question, 'Do you recognize this photograph?' Answer, 'I do. That was one of the men. I have never forgotten his face. I considered it to be an evil face. I was unable to sleep that night. I have often thought of it since.'"

"Excellent," said Petrella, who recognized hard evidence when he heard it.

"It's a great thought," said Dodds, "that in almost every street in London an old observant girl is sitting in a chair, in a bay window, noticing everything that goes on. All you've got to do is to find her."

"What are we going to do now?"

"We're waiting for a telephone call. As soon as it comes, we're going to start the ball rolling. I don't suppose we shall any of us get a lot of sleep tonight."

The call came at half past eight, and it was evidently satisfactory, for Kellaway appeared for a moment in the CID room to confer with Dodds.

"I'd better wait by the telephone," he said. "Then anyone who has got anything can reach me. Take Patrick with you. The exercise will do him good." He disappeared back into his room with a flash of his great white teeth.

Petrella could not afterwards have mapped out or set down the course they took that evening. It remained in his mind as a succession of sights and sounds and smells as they went from café to café and later, when the cafés were closed, from club to club. From private clubs to members' clubs, and finally to clubs so exclusive that they masqueraded as flats and apartments. The smells, particularly. The back alleys in which most of the clubs stood smelled of cats; and the clubs themselves of gin.

Their mission in these places, a mission which could sometimes be accomplished without actual eating or drinking, was to talk. Dodds did the talking. It was mostly in undertones, but in the end Petrella understood what was being said. The word was out against Howton. Information as to where he was lying would be paid for, in hard cash. And immunity from reprisals was absolutely guaranteed.

They visited Pino's and found Luard already busy. Evidently there were many workers in the field that night. Luard grinned at Petrella, and they plunged straight out again into the darkness. There was no time to waste on a place that was already covered.

And so the whisper ran, from street corner to street corner, from coffee stall to coffee stall. Telephones woke sleepy men in their beds who listened, and grunted. Many turned over and went to sleep again. A few decided that a stay in the country would suit their health and packed their bags and left London on very early trains.

At four o'clock in the morning, when the streets were quiet and the blood was thin, the telephone on Kellaway's desk sounded. He put down his cigarette quietly, balancing it on the rim of the ash-tray before he picked up the receiver. It was a woman's voice that spoke, briefly, without introduction or preamble. Kellaway, for his part, said nothing at all. When the woman had finished what she had to say, he replaced the receiver gently and got up from his chair. There was nothing in his movements to suggest that he had been sitting there, on and off, for seven hours. He walked across to the wall cupboard, opened it, and took out a new, soft black hat and placed it carefully on his head, the brim tilted very slightly forward and to the right.

Then he left the room, walked down into the courtyard, and woke up a dozing driver.

Ten minutes later he stopped the car at the end of a small street, spoke to the driver, who nodded, and got out, leaving the door open behind him. He walked along the pavement, his crêpe-soled shoes making no noise, and stopped at a doorway. As he got there, the door opened. A middle-aged woman, a dressing-gown round her shoulders, was crouching inside.

"First floor, back room," she said. "There's no lock on the door. The light switch is on the left as you go in. They promised – "

"Any promise that was made will be kept," said Kellaway. "Do your stairs creak?"

"Not a lot."

He went up them, drifted along the corridor, and threw open the end door, slamming down the light switch.

Boot Howton was up, on one elbow; but both his hands were visible.

"Get dressed," said Kellaway, "and come along."

8

The Magistrate Asks a Question

The barrister briefed by the director of public prosecutions was young and very painstaking. His wig was white and his soul was pure.

'There's no call to make heavy weather of it," said the head of his department. This is only the police court. You'll have Younger to lead you when you get to the Old Bailey."

"*If* we get to the Old Bailey," thought Mr Horsey, in a moment of panic, for it was his first big case. Two nights earlier he had woken his wife at midnight by sitting up in bed and beginning his opening speech. The next evening, being a woman of resource, she had slipped a couple of phenobarbitone tablets into his coffee.

"Your Worship," said Mr Horsey, "this is a case in which the Crown charges capital murder against the prisoner, Thomas Albert Howton."

"Capital murder, Mr Horsey?"

"That is so. Murder by shooting, contrary to subsection l(b) of Section 5 of the Homicide Act, 1957."

Even this arid formula could not conceal the real meaning of his words, and all eyes swivelled round, for an uncomfortable moment, to the man in the dock. The old beast of Capital Punishment had been driven into retreat, but here was one human being who still stood within reach of his claws.

"Very well, Mr Horsey," said the magistrate.

"It is my duty to adduce the evidence on which this charge is founded and to show a" – Mr Horsey swallowed briefly – "prima facie case for committal."

"I think we'd better have that window shut," said the magistrate. "Why the County Council must constantly operate a pneumatic drill when my court is sitting is something I have never been able to understand. Surely with a little co-operation they could do the work at weekends?"

The clerk said he would make a note of it.

The interruption enabled Mr Horsey to arrange his brief more conveniently, and he now proceeded with increasing confidence.

"The body of a woman, subsequently identified by the dental surgeon and the doctor who had treated her during her lifetime, as Mrs Rosa Ritchie, was discovered by some boys, lying among the bushes which overlook the Binford Park Reservoir, on the evening of November 5th."

"This year, or last year, Mr Horsey?"

"Oh, this year, sir."

"It's as well to be clear about these things."

Thus rebuked, Mr Horsey temporarily lost his place, but was given a further respite when the magistrate decided to have one of the radiators turned off.

Very gradually, as a small boat, its mast bent, its sail taut, will make headway on a succession of short tacks and violent jibes, so did Mr Horsey manage to unfold the prosecution's story. An additional source of discomfort to him was the presence, in the bench in front, of the grizzled wig, tipped at a sharp angle over the leathery face of Mr Claude Wainwright, QC. Mr Wainwright had appeared from nowhere, at the last moment, and announced that he was instructed on behalf of the prisoner. With him, Mr Clayesmore.

This, felt Horsey, was unfair. He had been clearly given to understand that senior counsel were not to take any part in the preliminary proceedings. It was not that Wainwright had done anything or said anything, but the presence of his stringy neck and indestructible wig was an affront.

"It seemed unnecessary to produce the boys themselves as witnesses," concluded Mr Horsey, "since they immediately, and very properly, sent for help in the form of the police. I will therefore call, as my first witness, Detective Sergeant Petrella."

"Detective Sergeant Petrella," boomed the uniformed usher, and Petrella, who had up to this moment been sitting in the company of the other Crown witnesses, on a nine-inch wide, worn, pinewood bench in an adjoining room, now stepped through the door and took the stand.

He described briefly how he had found the body, how it lay, and how it appeared to him that some effort had been made to cover it with leaves. He mentioned the finding of the newspaper with its missing centre pages, and he produced a large-scale plan of the reservoir, which was handed up to the magistrate, who kept the court waiting for several minutes while he examined it the wrong way up.

"One or two more questions, Sergeant," said Mr Horsey, "relating to a later date in this investigation. Do you identify these six pieces of jewellery?"

Petrella agreed that he did so.

"Have they been identified as the property of Messrs Colegraves, Jewellers of Oxford Street?"

Mr Claude Wainwright's wig rose about two inches, vertically, and the magistrate said, "I think, Mr Horsey, you ought to call a representative of Messrs Colegraves on that."

"Certainly, sir," said Mr Horsey, blushing again. "I intend to do so. I merely wished to establish with this officer that the pieces of jewellery in question were noted in the police pawn list as the property of Messrs Colegraves."

"The alleged property of Messrs Colegraves," said Mr Wainwright.

"Very well," said Mr Horsey patiently, "the alleged property of Messrs Colegraves."

Petrella admitted that this was so, and described his two visits to Mr Robins' shop. Mr Wainwright did not cross-examine, and he was released. He departed through the doors at the rear of the court, waited until he judged that Mr Horsey had got his teeth into the next witness, and then came quietly back and slipped into one of the public benches. The uniformed policeman on duty saw him come in and winked at him.

He had never really appreciated before what a very large number of witnesses, most of them quite unimportant, the law demanded before it would accept the simplest fact.

The next man in the box was the draftsman from New Scotland Yard who had actually drawn the plan to which Petrella had referred. There followed the compiler of the pawn list, a representative of Messrs Colegraves, Mr Robins, and Mr Robins' son, Richard.

Claude Wainwright, who had been apparently asleep, now woke up for a moment.

"When you were asked to identify the man who, it is suggested, had deposited these articles with you some time previously," he said, "how was the matter transacted?"

Young Robins, who had lost his bearings about halfway through the question, gaped at him.

"I mean," said Mr Wainwright, "what happened? Did the police officer produce Howton to you in person, eh?"

"Oh, no, sir."

"Showed you photographs then?"

"That's right, sir. He had a photograph."

"I've no doubt," said Mr Wainwright, "that being a conscientious officer, who knew his duty, he showed you six or eight different photographs and asked you to pick out from them the person you recognized?"

"Well, no, sir. He just showed me one."

"Indeed," said Mr Wainwright. "And what did he say? Did he say, 'That's the man who left the jewellery here, isn't it?' "

"I can't remember exactly what he did say."

"Something like that?"

"Yes, sir."

Mr Wainwright subsided into his gown like an old, tired balloon deflating.

The next witness was Dr Summerson. He told, in his high-pitched, impersonal voice, of the finding of the body, of his observations as to the probable time it had been there, of the autopsy subsequently conducted by him in the Highside Mortuary, and of his conclusion that Mrs Ritchie had been killed by a bullet, fired from a pistol actually pressed against her body.

"I removed," he concluded, "from the neighborhood of the spinal column, at a point seven inches below the fourth cervical vertebra, a cupronickel-cased lead bullet which I placed in a plastic envelope. I sealed and initialled the envelope and subsequently handed it to Superintendent Causton of the Forensic Science Laboratory at New Scotland Yard together with certain other exhibits."

Dr Summerson proceeded to detail in precise tones, which somehow robbed his words of offense, exactly those portions of poor Mrs Ritchie that he had removed, labelled and handed to Superintendent Causton. At the moment when he seemed to be about to step down from the box, Mr Horsey asked, "Were there any other points of general interest about your examination which might assist the court?"

"My examination," said Dr Summerson, "also revealed that the deceased was three months pregnant at the time of her death."

The reporters' pencils scurried and squeaked. Summerson was always news. And here, at least, was a simple fact. Something that the reading public could grasp, and speculate about. The woman had been found in November. Her husband went to prison – when? About the previous Christmas. Now they were getting somewhere.

Disappointingly, Mr Wainwright seemed unmoved and unsurprised. He broke off a low-voiced conversation with Mr Clayesmore long enough to indicate that he had no questions to ask, and Dr Summerson stepped smartly from the box and was driven off in the direction of Greys Hospital, where he was due to deliver a lecture on gallstones as an aid to identification.

His place was taken by Superintendent Causton, who deposed that he had handed over the bullet handed to him by Dr Summerson to another authority for microphotographic examination, and he, in turn, was replaced by Charles Fenwick ("the well-known ballistics expert"), who expressed the view that the bullet found in the body had been fired from a *P*38 pistol, a high-velocity weapon used by the German Army.

"Normally," said Mr Horsey, "a bullet fired from such a weapon might pass right through the body of the person it struck?"

Mr Fenwick agreed that it might, but said that if the pistol were actually pressed against the body of the victim, as Dr Summerson had suggested, this would decrease its momentum and velocity.

Mr Fenwick then described, in considerable detail, a series of experiments he had made, by firing bullets from a *P*38 pistol handed to him (Exhibit Six) and discovered, so he understood, adjacent to the scene of the crime.

At the end of all this Mr Wainwright rose to his feet and observed that the defence did not intend to contest the fact that the bullet found in the deceased's body had been fired from the automatic pistol (Exhibit Six). It occurred to Petrella that if he had said so earlier, it would have saved everyone a lot of time and trouble but Mr Horsey seemed to be gratified by the admission.

"I now propose," he said, "to deal with the question of identity."

"After lunch," said the magistrate, and rose to his feet and disappeared. The court emptied. Petrella wanted time for thought, and ate a solitary meal at a snack bar round the corner. There were, no doubt, a number of little routine jobs which he could have been doing, but technically he was still engaged, full time, on the Rosa Ritchie case and he could think of no more useful place to study that case in its entirety than the back of the Highside Magistrate's Court.

In the somnolent hour which followed lunch the court disposed of Mrs Ritchie's doctor and dentist, who were able to set at rest, from their careful records, any doubts as to identity. After them came Mrs Fraser.

"It was with this witness," explained Mr Horsey, "that the deceased was lodging at the time she met her death. She was the first person to identify her, but her evidence, as to clothing and shoes and so on, is not, perhaps, necessary in view of the witnesses you have just heard."

The magistrate agreed that this was so.

"I shall ask her, then, first to tell us what she can about the deceased's movements on the day she met her death."

"Is presumed to have met her death," said Mr Wainwright. "We have at the moment no evidence on the point beyond an evening paper, which, even if it belonged to the deceased, she may easily have purchased some days before and carried about with her."

Mr Horsey's mind was not flexible enough to deal, on the spot, with the possibilities opened up by this comment, so he merely repeated submissively, "Very well – is presumed to have met her death. Now, Mrs Fraser – ?"

There was not, after all, a great deal that she could tell. Rosa had not left the flat when she herself went out to work. That would have been before half past eight. She had to be at work by nine. Being Saturday, she had her lunch at a place near her work, did some shopping, and got home about three. Rosa was gone. Her handbag and coat and hat were gone, but there was nothing to show that her departure was intended to be permanent.

"But in fact you never saw her again."

"Never."

"She had her own key?"

"She had a front-door key and a flat key."

"Which were found in her handbag and later identified by you?"

"Yes."

"Was she often out late at night?"

"Yes."

"Sometimes all night?"

"Oh, yes."

"Did you ever ask her where she had been?"

"Certainly not, why should I?"

"No reason at all," agreed Mr Horsey. "Only, if you had asked her, and she had told you, it might have been interesting for us to know."

This did not appear to be a question, so the witness made no attempt to answer it.

"I should like you to look at the accused."

Mrs Fraser twisted round and looked unwillingly at Howton, who glared back at her out of his single eye.

"Have you ever seen him before today?"

"Once or twice, yes."

"In what circumstances?"

It was clear that she was pausing to choose her words.

"He seemed to be some sort of acquaintance of Rosa's."

"Someone she was intimate with?"

"Really!" Mr Wainwright exploded like an expensive cracker.

"I meant, was he an intimate friend?"

"Intimacy, Mr Horsey," said the magistrate, "is a word which, when used in court, for some reason I have never been able to understand, almost always implies impropriety. Is that what you are alleging?"

It was clearly what Mr Horsey would have liked to allege; it was also quite clearly outside his brief, so he shook his head sulkily.

"If not," continued the magistrate, "I would suggest that you merely ask the witness to describe what occurred within her own observation."

It amounted, again, to very little. Howton had called once or twice. She could not be pinned down to dates, but certainly not more than six times during the period that Rosa had lodged with her.

"And were any of those the occasions on which she failed to return until the following morning?" inquired the magistrate.

"No. She was back within a few hours on those occasions."

Mr Horsey looked cross and said he had no more questions. Mr Wainwright looked pleased, and indicated that he, too, would leave well alone. As the witness was on the point of descending and the usher had actually taken a deep breath to shout for the next witness, the magistrate raised his hand. He was a very shrewd old man, wise by experience rather than book reading in the ways of the law. He could read the minds of both counsel with precision. Both were afraid of asking any more questions lest they prejudice their position at the later hearing. He was servant to no such hopes or fears.

"I would like to be a little clearer about this, Mrs Fraser," he said. "It is a matter of some importance, you know. You are describing the relationship between the woman who is dead and the man who is accused of her murder. Would you have described them as lovers?"

Mrs Fraser thought about it. Then she said, "Not in the film sense."

"You mean there was nothing romantic about it?"

"Definitely not."

"But there could have been a more sordid relationship."

"Yes. I suppose so. There could have been."

"I am not here to put words into your mouth, Mrs Fraser. You are a woman of the world. Just how would you describe it yourself?"

"I should say that it was – a sort of business relationship between them."

The magistrate turned it over in his mind. The packed court was completely silent. Petrella found that the palms of his hands were wet. It was extraordinary how the bumbling processes of the law could roll along, hour after hour, producing nothing, and then, suddenly, a witness would say something that opened up a vista of startling clarity.

"Very well, Mrs Fraser," said the magistrate.

The rest of the evidence was something of an anticlimax. Mrs Gurney told of seeing the accused near the reservoir on the night of September 22nd. The young man who had been in charge of the diving operation, and whose name turned out to be William Borden, gave evidence of the finding of a *P*38 pistol in the reservoir and reidentified Exhibit Six. He was of the opinion that it was a good deal too far from any point on the bank to have been thrown. In his view it had been dropped from a boat. This brought on Sergeant Dodds, who told of the finding of the boat, on the far bank of the reservoir. No one could offer any explanation as to why, if the murderer had rowed out in the boat to dispose of the pistol, he had not simply rowed back again and left it in its shed; and Mr Wainwright made a number of sharp notes on his brief.

The next witness was a man whom Petrella had not seen before. He had an indefinable air of spuriousness about him, which was apparent even before he opened his mouth and increased when he did so. He gave his name as Charles Garden, his occupation as an agent, and an address in Paddington. He spoke of an incident, in a club in Scrope Street, when the accused had been present and had produced an automatic pistol which, in Mr Garden's opinion, was the same as Exhibit Six.

Mr Wainwright rose to his feet and addressed the magistrate, not the witness. He wished, he said, to protest in the strongest manner possible against the last-minute inclusion of Garden among the prosecution witnesses. His name had not appeared in the original list, and he had therefore had no opportunity of checking his character and standing.

The magistrate said he was sure that the prosecution, now they had called him, would give Mr Wainwright every possible opportunity of examining the witness' credentials. Mr Wainwright said he hoped so. And the witness disappeared with a speed which suggested that he was happy to get out of the box.

His place was taken by Superintendent Kellaway, who supplied some badly needed background. He told the court of the escape of Monk Ritchie from custody and his presumed departure to France. He described his investigations at the reservoir and at the cottage ("At that time, standing empty"), culminating in the discovery of a complete set of fingerprints on the window jamb ("as to which," he understood, "a later witness would speak"). As he quitted the box, having left out, Petrella thought, a great deal more than he had put in, the magistrate glanced at the clock. It was five minutes to five.

"If you have many more witnesses – " he said to Mr Horsey.

"In fact, your Worship, only one more. Superintendent Burrell of the Fingerprint Section at New Scotland Yard."

"Very well," said the magistrate. "I am myself quite prepared, of course, to sit here until any hour, but I have my officials to think about."

The superintendent stepped up into the box, and was soon deep in the complexities of his craft. The atmosphere thickened as loops, arches, whorls and composites, outer termini, closed deltas, and secondary characteristics flowed in a steady stream over the long-suffering heads of the magistrate's clerk and his shorthand typist, who were the people chiefly responsible for reducing to intelligible compass the depositions of the witnesses.

The clock was pointing to half past five when the magistrate said, "I take it, Superintendent, that what you are telling us is that you, as an expert, are perfectly satisfied that the four finger-prints on the cottage window were made by the prisoner?"

"That is so, sir."

Now, thought Petrella. Now for it.

"Have you anything to add, Superintendent?"

"No, sir. I think that is all."

"Any more questions, Mr Horsey?"

He *can't,* thought Petrella. He can't. Even Kellaway. He can't get away with it.

"No more questions," said Mr Horsey, his voice now reduced to a croak.

"Have you any submissions on the evidence, Mr Wainwright?"

Mr Wainwright said that he was instructed to reserve his defence for a subsequent occasion. This was not to be construed as meaning that he agreed in any way with the evidence as put forward.

"In that case," said the magistrate, "I have to record that I find a prima facie case made out against the accused. And I shall order that he be committed for trial at the session of the London Assizes commencing at the Central Criminal Court in three weeks' time. Copies of all depositions to be made available to the defence."

Petrella missed the closing formalities. He was out in the streets again, walking furiously. Hard as he walked, he could not outwalk his thoughts.

9

A Bolshevik Conspiracy

"I'm not saying," said Superintendent Kellaway, "that I don't sympathize with you." He looked hard at Petrella, who was standing stiffly in front of his desk. "But this is my case, I'm responsible for it from the moment I'm put in charge until the jury files out at the Old Bailey. After that, you can do what you like about it."

Petrella said, "I only thought, it might have been safer, from our point of view, to tell them about the print on the gun. The Fingerprint Section at Central are working on it now. Suppose it turns out to be someone not connected with Howton at all. It'd mean a last-minute switch in the case. Mightn't that be more awkward than having it now?"

"If it turned out to be Charlie Chaplin," said Kellaway, "it wouldn't make a farthing's worth of difference to my case. That's one thing you've got to learn about police work, son. Concentrate on what does matter. Cut out what doesn't. You try to put forward all the facts, and what happens? Someone on the jury thinks up some theory or other, and once the jury get hold of a pet theory of their own, you can whistle for a conviction."

Petrella was well aware of the tricky nature of the ground on which he was treading. He was also perfectly conscious of the proper relationship between a junior detective sergeant and a senior and experienced detective superintendent, a man who, in the normal course of promotion, would next be given charge of a district; and who might therefore – the chances were, after all, only three to one against it – become Petrella's next chief.

Nevertheless, there was something which had to be said.

"You'll have to put it down to ignorance, sir. But I thought the prosecution had to give all the evidence to the defence. Whether it made sense or not. It's not only the second finger-print. I mean the fact that Ricketts left his cottage that day and has never been seen again. It could be a coincidence. Or he might have been meaning to go for some time. And hearing the shooting and all that rumpus, he got frightened, and pulled out straight away. Or – "

"Or he might be in the reservoir too," said Kellaway softly. "Yes? I've thought of that too. With the second bullet in him? Right?"

Petrella nodded.

"Now tell me this: what difference would it make to the case against Howton if he knocked off Ricketts as well – because he got in the way or to stop him talking? We're not charging him with two murders. Why should we? One's enough to hang him." He paused, then added, "Did you know that Charlie Gover is still unconscious, and every hour he's out makes it less likely he'll ever come round again? Even if he does he may be blind, or paralyzed, or plain crazy. That's the sort of thing a boot in the head does for you."

Petrella nodded. He had no answer to this.

"When you're fighting a war, you stick to the rules – if you can. But if the rules get in the way of winning, you toss 'em overboard. And with people like Howton I'm at war. As for giving the defence all the evidence, the rules say we must answer all their questions, fully and truthfully. I'll do that. If anyone asks me about the print on the gun, I'll tell 'em. But not before. The same with Ricketts. One thing you said about that made sense. It might have been a coincidence. They're things that happen quite a lot in real life. I once arrested a man for a murder he did for £75, on the same day that he won the Treble Chance Pool first dividend of £75,000."

Kellaway got up, came round, and added, in tones of surprising friendliness, "Anyway, it's something I've got to worry about, not you. Until the case finishes one way or the other, at the Bailey, you're under my orders. And I'm ordering you not to worry about it. You can have it in writing if you like."

"No, that's all right, sir," said Petrella, summoning up a smile of his own. "I won't ask you to commit it to writing."

After he had gone, Kellaway sat for a few minutes, quite still and perfectly relaxed. Then he rang the bell for Sergeant Dodds.

Petrella walked out of Crown Road Police Station in a bad temper. He had been cleverly handled, and the fact that he knew it did not make it any better. The appeal which had been made to him was a hard one to deny. The police were a private army. Criminals were the enemy. The rest of the world were onlookers. Onlookers with certain undefined but unpleasant powers of interference. The way to deal with them was to stick to the letter of the law. Learn the Judges' Rules by heart, and give the devil no more than his due. And over all, and before all, and above all, never forget that the team came first.

And if he did decide to do the unspeakable thing, whose side was he on? On Boot Howton's – who had kicked Charlie Gover nearly to death, who bullied and pimped and tramped on people weaker than himself. A creature who, in a rational society, would be put away. Was he going to fight for him and against (not Kellaway, Kellaway was an accident, something that had happened to him) – against Gwilliam and Gover and Haxtell?

"I'm damned if I'll do it," said Petrella out loud.

"Certainly not," said someone behind him. Petrella swung about, and found the face of Mr William Borden a few inches from his.

"Oh, hullo," said Petrella. "I'm sorry. I don't usually talk to myself."

"You look pretty steamed up," said Borden. "Come and have a noggin. They're just open."

"Good idea," said Petrella. He drank very little, and never at midday, but this seemed the moment to start a few bad habits.

"There's a pub here," said Borden, "that's got a shove ha'penny board with a set of original William and Mary shillings. They're polished smooth on one side, but you can read the superscription on the other side quite easily. Did you know that the game originated in the reign of Queen Elizabeth the First? God bless her. The beer's not at all bad, either."

The beer was very good, light amber brown, well cooled and of greater than ordinary strength. They drank a pint each, slowly, and a second pint rather faster. The third pint they carried across to a table in the corner of the empty bar.

"The trouble with everyone nowadays," said Borden, "is that they're too nice. Did we create the greatest country in the world by being nice? Did we win every war from 1066 onwards – except the War of American Independence, but I don't count that, they cheated – by being nice? Did we found the British Empire by being nice? Like hell we did. We starved and bullied and flogged our children until they ran away from home, and went off and conquered India."

He took a further draught of beer and added, "Nowadays, all our virtues are negative ones. Hurt no one. Be fair to everybody. Save money. Don't take risks."

"Is it easy to be a frogman?" said Petrella, who was following his own thoughts, as people often do when they are drinking together.

"Nothing to it. Teach you in the morning."

"Isn't it dangerous?"

"Only if you forget to put enough warm clothes on. Could catch a nasty cold. A friend of mine got pneumonia, diving without his pants on. Now, there's another thing. That job we were on at the reservoir. When we found the gun – you remember?"

"Yes, I remember."

"Do you know why we stopped?"

"I thought you'd finished."

"Finished nothing. We were less than halfway across. What they *said* was, to save money. We're an expensive outfit. Set you back twenty-five quid a day for our services. All right. We'd found what they were looking for, so we stop. Economy. But that wasn't the real reason. Another pint?"

"I – oh, yes. If you like."

The fourth pint was brought.

Petrella said, "What you were saying about that reservoir job. Why *did* you stop?"

"We stopped because they were bloody scared that we might turn up something else and spoil the case they were cobbling up. I'm sorry to say it, Patrick. But sometimes I'm afraid the police stink."

"That's all right," said Petrella. "Don't mind me. The real thing is, are you prepared to do anything about it?"

"I'm prepared to do anything about anything."

"Do you mean that?"

"Are you calling me a bloody liar?"

"No. Certainly not. But people do sometimes say they're going to do things and then not do them. I'm sure," added Petrella hastily, "that you're not like that."

"What do you suggest we do?" said Borden, suddenly becoming reasonable and businesslike.

"I think the same as you do. There's something more in that reservoir. Maybe another gun. Maybe – something quite different."

"Maybe the old boy who lived in the cottage and walked out of it without leaving a forwarding address."

"Yes."

"And you'd like me to have a shot at finding him for you?"

"What I'd really like to do is have a shot myself, with you to show me how, I mean."

"This calls for more beer."

"It's my turn." Petrella secured two more pints. It was the nicest beer he remembered drinking. It was a pity that he spilled a bit of it on the return journey, but the floor had a very slight tilt. He hadn't noticed it before. "I suppose you can do that diving stuff after dark?"

"Certainly. Electric torch on the helmet. Matter of fact, it's always dark if you go deep enough."

"We'd have to do it at night, anyway. Otherwise we'd give the show away. Even if we slipped in without being seen, people would spot bubbles from the what's-its-name."

"From the aqualung. Yes. There is an oxygen set, which doesn't show bubbles. But the aqualung's safer."

"I'd have to practice quite a bit first," said Petrella.

"The best place for that's a swimming pool." Borden felt for his wallet and extracted a card. "That's got my business telephone number on it. If you feel of the same mind tomorrow morning, ring me up. How are we going to square this with the top brass?"

"I don't," said Petrella with dignity, "anticipate any trouble at all."

"You don't, eh?"

"None at all. If Superintendent Kellaway says anything to me, I shall say to him, 'Fiat justitia, ruat coelum'."

"That ought to shake him," agreed Borden. "What does it mean?"

"It means," said Petrella, " 'Let justice prevail, though the sky fall.' "

"I see." Borden looked at his new friend critically. "And just when were you planning to say this?"

"The next time he says something to me."

"I think I should leave it until tomorrow if I was you. It'll sound all the better in the morning." He got up and walked slowly across to the door, Petrella following him willy-nilly.

Outside the sun was shining and the sky was blue.

"What about something to eat?"

"No," said Petrella. "No time. Too busy to eat."

"What about a taxi?"

"Perfectly all right," said Petrella. "Very good of you, but perfectly all right. Be seeing you." He swung round on his heel, went rather farther than he had intended, and steadied himself by holding onto the lamp-post.

"Hell's bells," said Borden to himself.

As he watched, Petrella smiled gravely at him, waved, and started straight off down the pavement, did a stem turn at the corner, and disappeared from his sight.

"At least he can still walk," said Borden. "Stupid of me really. I hope he'll be all right."

Petrella felt fine. It was a grand day. He was in grand form. The world was a good place. All that was needed was a little give and take, a little co-operation. Why had this not occurred to him before? Now that it had occurred to him, he would put it into practice. He would seek out Superintendent Kellaway, and he would say –

"Where are you off to, Patrick?"

Sergeant Gwilliam loomed up in front of him.

"I'm going to see Superintendent Kellaway and I'm going to talk to him about co-opper-operation."

"Are you, now?" said Gwilliam thoughtfully. He waved his hand, and the police car which had been idling by the curb drew up.

"It's a house at the top of Foljamb Road. No. 37, I think."

"There's a mistake somewhere here," said Petrella. "I don't want to go home. I want to go to the station. I've got something important I must say to old Kellaway."

He found himself in the back of the car with Sergeant Gwilliam wedged in beside him. At 37 Foljamb Road, where Petrella's landlady, Mrs Catt, lived, he protested again, but feebly. The front door was open, and Gwilliam came in with him.

"Which is your room?" he said. "First floor back. All right. Up we go. Less talk and a little more co-opper-operation."

Next morning Petrella woke feeling curiously clear-headed and with an imprecise recollection of the previous day. He remembered Bill Borden, and took out his card and looked at it.

One of the police drivers grinned at him as he went in. He found Gwilliam at work.

"Did you take me home in a car yesterday?"

"That's right," said Gwilliam. "You had a touch of flu."

Later that day he had to go down to Scotland Yard, and he called in on Sergeant Blinder to see how he was progressing.

"You want to know about that print on the gun," said the sergeant. "That's not so easy. It's a single print. Quite a good-looking one, as I said." He pulled out a ten-magnification photograph and Petrella stared uncomprehendingly at the ridges and valleys, the watersheds and river junctions of the human tegument. It might have been a physical geography of the moon for all it said to him.

"You've got six to eight possible points of identification. But nothing so absolutely out of the way that you can make a positive start from it."

"You mean that if it had a scar across it, or something like that, you could use that as a short cut?"

"We'll clear it in time," said Blinder. "Don't you worry. We can't work miracles, that's all. No matter who calls for 'em."

Petrella gathered that Kellaway had been exercising some more of his well-known drive on the Fingerprint Section.

"I tell 'em all," said Sergeant Blinder, "that fingerprints are a science. You can't hustle science. Not if you want reliable results."

"Tell me something," said Petrella. "Do you have all your prints in a single collection?"

"That's right. One main index of all recorded prints. Except, of course, there's the Aged Collection."

"Aged Collection?"

"Prints over a certain age. We don't keep 'em in the main index forever."

"What's the time limit?"

"There's no rule. But if a print hasn't been turned up for thirty or forty years we take the view that the owner's seen the light of reason and decided to behave himself. Have you got any reason to think – ?"

"No," said Petrella. "There aren't any old-age pensioners involved in this case. All the same – suppose a man did something silly when he was seventeen. Forty years later he'd be fifty-seven. Not too old to beat up some more trouble if he wanted to."

"All right," said Blinder. "Better safe than sorry. When I've cleared the main index I'll sort out the old-age pensioners for you as well."

That evening Petrella completed the first part of his programme by calling at No. 39 Corum Street. Mrs Fraser was in all right. He could hear her moving about. But there was a long interval after he knocked, and at first he wondered if she would answer at all.

Eventually, when she had identified her caller, she slipped the catch and let him in.

"You can't stay long," she said. "What is it you want?"

"Can I sit down?"

"Yes, of course." She summoned up a smile for him. It was about as warm and heartfelt as a chairman's annual vote of thanks to the staff.

"I'll try not to bother you. I expect you've been bothered enough in the past few days."

She looked up sharply at this.

"Giving evidence in court."

"Oh, *that*. I didn't mind that. I thought the magistrate was rather nice. Did you hear me?"

"I was in the back row of the stalls," said Petrella. "I thought you gave a most polished performance."

She smiled again, a little more happily.

"What do you want to know now?"

"It's a matter of timing that's been worrying me. You know Rosa's husband, Monk Ritchie, got away from his prison escort on the Friday. It happened in the early afternoon."

"Did it? I don't think that was in the papers."

"I'm telling you," said Petrella. "And please get it out of your head that I'm trying to trap you or trip you up in some way. I'm telling you because I want your help."

"All right."

"What I was thinking was this. We've all been assuming that Monk lay up, that first night, with Howton and the other boys. And I expect he did. But it seems to me, don't you think, that he would have tried to get hold of his wife first?"

"Yes, I suppose so."

"That would be on Friday evening. He wouldn't come here, of course. He'd know the place would be watched as soon as his escape was notified. It would have to be a telephone message. What arrangement have you got about those?"

"There's a telephone in the basement, where the woman who owns the house hangs out. She's not keen on us bothering her, so we don't encourage our friends to ring us up. In all the time I've been here, I doubt I've been rung up twice."

"In that case," said Petrella, "it would be likely to stick in your mind if anyone telephoned Rosa that Friday evening."

"Yes," said Mrs Fraser. "It would stick in my memory."

"And did they?"

In the sudden silence Petrella could pick up the sound of movement in the next room. Evidently the Polish lady was at home.

"If you don't remember, I could ask the lady in the basement."

"No. I'd rather you didn't do that. She's very touchy. I'm casting my mind back. There *was* a call."

"You're certain?"

"Yes. Fairly certain. It would be about nine o'clock that night."

"Was Mrs Ritchie away long?"

"I don't think so, or I should have remembered."

"And did you notice any difference in her manner when she came back?"

Jean made a little gesture of impatience. "We weren't sharing rooms," she said. "She was living her life, I was living mine. I know she had this call, and I know when she went out and when she came back, because she had to come through my room. If she'd had a door of her own, I wouldn't have known anything much about her at all."

"I quite see that," said Petrella, "and I'm sorry to have bothered you. You've made the last question I wanted to ask you unnecessary as well." He took up his hat.

"That's a neat way to tantalize a body. Now I shall lie awake all night wondering what it was."

"It was just a thought really," said Petrella. "I wondered if Mrs Ritchie might have known Ricketts?"

"Who was Ricketts?"

"He was an intake attendant," said Petrella. "It's all right. I can let myself out. Good night."

He closed the door softly. Mrs Fraser stood still, her head bent, listening to his footsteps tip-tapping down the stairs, then across the bare linoleum of the hall. She heard the front door slam and still she made no move.

10

Progress of the Conspiracy

"When you come to working out of doors, in weather like this," said Bill Borden, "you'll put on everything you've got. String vest, long pants, pullover, balaclava helmet, socks, mittens. Just for practising in a heated swimming bath, a pair of bathing trunks will do."

"What a lot of stuff," said Petrella.

"It's all useful. Put on the bottom part of the suit first. You have to wriggle a bit to get your legs right down. OK? Now I'll put on mine. Then we can help each other into our tops. This sort of thing's always better done in pairs. I dived for years with a chap called Dickie Farragut."

"What happened to him?"

"He got married, and went into breakfast food. Now for a bit of deflation."

As he spoke he was unrolling a length of tubing which was attached halfway down the front of the suit.

"Just like an umbilical cord," said Petrella.

"Same thing, but in reverse," said Borden. "This is used for extraction." He put the end of the tube in his mouth and started to suck. Petrella followed suit. At once he could feel the rubber diving suit begin to tighten against his flesh. It was a not unpleasant sensation, like growing a new skin.

"Most important part of the operation," said Borden, between gasps. "Must empty all the air out of a suit before you start. If you don't, as likely as not it goes down to your heels. Nothing makes you feel sillier than bumping round on your forehead. Now roll the tube up and tuck it in. Same principle as when you fasten up a football, only this time you're inside the ball. Next the aqualung. Test it before you put it on."

"Test *what?*"

"Just give it a couple of sucks to see the air's coming through. If the intake valve sticks, you'll have to surface in a hurry. Set the regulator at five. Now put her up on your back. Like a haversack. Gloves and flippers next, and you're practically ready to go."

He examined the new recruit critically.

"All you need's your weight belt."

"I feel quite heavy enough already, thank you."

"If you went into the water like that, you'd float, not sink. The compressed air in that aqualung's as good as a Mae West." Borden extracted from the kit bag a broad webbing belt with slots in it and, after some thought, inserted eight flat leaden discs. "It's a funny thing, but in the early days it always used to be assumed that you had to put the weights in the *feet*. Sort of hangover from the days of diving suits. Made swimming almost impossible. That's right. The torch on your helmet may make a bit of difference. I'll adjust you after the first dive if you feel at all sluggish."

"I don't feel sluggish," said Petrella. "I feel immobile."

"Just wait till you get in the water."

"Dive in?"

"Nothing so dashing. Lower yourself in sedately, bottom first. If you dived, as like as not you'd tear the mask right off your face. All set?"

Petrella lowered himself obediently into the water, clung onto the rail for a moment, and then let go. His trim had been so accurately adjusted that he felt neither weight nor buoyancy. It was only when his world showed suddenly green that he realized he was under the surface. He turned over, steadied himself, and then shot across the floor of the bath, with such speed that he nearly crashed head-on into the wall opposite. He saved himself with his hands, and came more sedately back again. Nothing to it, really.

After five minutes he surfaced, and found Borden sitting on the edge of the pool smoking a cigarette.

"Is that all?"

"In six foot of water in a warmed and lighted swimming pool, yes," said Borden. "The next thing you've got to practise is just getting the stuff off and on, until you can do it blindfolded. Remember, next time you put it on will be in the dark, in the open. And it'll probably be raining. When you can get properly rigged up inside ten minutes in conditions like that you'll be fit for fieldwork. Now, let's start from the beginning again – "

That evening, after dark, they made a reconnaissance of the reservoir. Borden parked his car in a cul-de-sac south of the Binford Park Sports Ground. He had the diving gear in two large duffel bags. They found, without much difficulty, a place where they could climb the railings, and started up. By keeping the embanked running track on their left and working along the inner fence which separated it from the reservoir, they had no difficulty in locating the gate, now embellished with a shiny new padlock.

"Lucky I kept a spare key," said Petrella, with a grin. The old iron gate squeaked in protest as they opened it,

"Needs a spot of oil," said Borden. "I'll remember to bring some next time. This is only a dry run. Just to see what the snags are. What we want now's a changing room. We *can* do it in the open, but we may have to use torches, and we don't want someone spotting us and dialling 999."

"What about the cottage? Then we could go in from the landing stage."

"Not a bad idea," said Borden. "Really, quite a good idea. Do you think we can get in without busting anything?"

"I noticed the window in the scullery had a fairly simple slip catch."

It proved easier even than that. The kitchen door was unlocked.

"Would there be any risk, do you think," said Borden, "if we actually keep our stuff here? It would save us humping it up each night."

It was a novel idea, but its attractions were obvious.

"How long do you reckon this is going to take us?"

"Five or six nights to do the thing properly. An aqualung lasts about two hours. I don't reckon we could do much more than an hour a night. Apart from anything else, the cold gets you down in the end."

"Then we've got to take a chance on no one having occasion to search this place for a week."

"That's right."

"I think it's a fair bet. The only people likely to be nosing about are the Water Board. Suppose they find our suits. Ten to one old Lundgren will assume it's something official, to do with the police, and he'll contact me."

"Fair enough. Let's get going."

As they left the cottage the moon came out from behind a slow-moving cloud and silvered the picture for them. A light mist was lying on the surface of the reservoir. The water looked black and cold and as tenacious in its mystery as the grave itself.

"Do you mean to say," said Petrella in a whisper, "that we have got to look inside that?"

"Cold feet?"

"Cold all over."

It took half an hour to shift the gear. They found a big cupboard in the kitchen, wide enough to store the kit bags, end to end, on the floor. As Petrella was fitting them into place, something drove painfully into the index finger of his right hand.

"Ouch," he said.

Borden turned the torch on. "You been bitten by a rat?"

"No. It feels like the broken end of a nail."

"Better get that cleaned up," said Borden. Blood was beginning to ooze. "A friend of mine lost his right hand just that way. A rusty nail – "

MICHAEL GILBERT

"You and your friends," said Petrella. "Don't worry about my hand. Shine the torch on the floor. I want to see what did it."

It was the broken end of a brass screw; possibly the shaft of a cup hook which had been driven in too hard and snapped off.

"Funny place to hang a cup," said Borden.

"Have you a screwdriver?"

There was one in the frogman's kit. Petrella wrapped a handkerchief round his hand to staunch the blood, which was now flowing freely from the gash in his finger, put the end of the screwdriver into the join in the floor a few inches from the broken shank of the hook, and levered. A piece of floorboard came up.

Borden was breathing down his neck.

"What is it?"

"It's a cache. Something someone used to keep things in. He's sawed off one end of the board. See? Not very long ago. Then, as it was a tight fit, he used to drive a cup hook in to lift it out with. Then the hook broke. And now I cut my finger on it."

It was a space perhaps three feet long, and nine inches wide, blocked off on two sides by the brick wall and on the other two by joists. And it was empty.

Petrella put the board back and stood up. In the moment of silence which followed they both heard the slither and bump. There was some kind of furtive animal life under the floorboards and behind the wainscoting.

"Do you know," said Borden, "there's something I don't quite like about this place. Difficult to say what. It just doesn't feel right."

Petrella said. "It's the damp. You can smell it."

"It smells worse than damp to me," said Borden. "Let's get back to the car before we start imagining things."

On the following evening Petrella came off duty at seven o'clock. His plans were to have an early evening meal, and then to relax until it was time to meet Borden, which he was due to do at eleven o'clock in the cul-de-sac where the car was parked.

As he turned into Foljamb Road, a figure drifted up out of the shadows between two street lamps. It was a girl. Petrella had never seen her before. She looked, in the dim light, to be about seventeen. She had a sick, white face and she spoke with the husky voice of a heavy smoker.

"Your name Pirelli?"

"Petrella."

"That's it. You're a bogey."

"I'm a bogey," agreed Petrella gravely, as one might say to a little girl, "I'm Father Christmas."

"Got a message from Jean. She wants to see you."

"Now?"

"No. And you're not to come to her place. That's important. Not to come to her place, nor where she works."

"Then how?"

"You know Collins' shop?"

Petrella reflected. "Yes," he said at last. "A little newsagent and tobacconist in Canal Street."

" 'Sright. She'll put a card in the window when she can see you. You watch out for it."

"What's your name?" said Petrella. But he found he was talking to himself and the lamp-post. The girl had gone.

Petrella went home. Mrs Catt was an excellent cook and understood the appetite of a young man who spent most of a long working day on his feet in the open air. After dinner he settled down with *Reese on Play*, to study the tactics of the throw-in.

It was a little difficult, at first, until you grasped the underlying principle. Once you had that firmly in your mind, it was simple. You were sitting South. North, you were not surprised to find, was Superintendent Kellaway. Dodds was East and Gover, looking a little pale after his stay in hospital, was West. Now, then, play out all the clubs. Then all the diamonds except one. What would you have left? Petrella was disconcerted to find that there was nothing at all in his hands except photographs of fingerprints, and from somewhere behind him Sergeant Blinder was saying, "Take a central pocket loop whorl with an inner tracing", when his head fell forward, sharply, making him bite his tongue. He came slowly back to the present and examined the clock. It was a quarter past ten, and time to think about getting ready if he wasn't to be late at the rendezvous.

At eleven o'clock exactly, Borden's car turned the corner, cut its engine, and drifted to a stop. Petrella was waiting. There was no need for talk. It took ten minutes to reach the cottage. The threads that Petrella had stretched across the back door and the cupboard were unbroken. Their base was secure.

Borden had brought blankets with him, and these they nailed across the single small window. A candle was brought, and by its dancing light the ceremony of dressing began. It was a rite they were to carry out six times in all, and the memory of it remained in Petrella's mind when a lot else had faded. If some passer-by, attracted by a chink of light at the window, had crept up and peered in, what would he have seen? What would he have done? Run screaming, doubtless, at the sight of the great, black, contorted shapes of men from outer space, glass-masked, hunchbacked, web-footed, their black hands performing strange rituals.

Curiously enough, all feeling of nightmare receded as soon as Petrella entered the water. This was a job of work. Something which needed proper attention and left no room for fantasy.

Borden submerged first, to mark the area of their night's search with long aluminum pegs. They were starting where the official search had left off, casting wide on either side of the line.

"I'll mark out an oblong strike," said Borden. "You work up and down the left-hand side, from the corners, inwards to the centre pegs. I'll do the same on the right-hand side. Don't hurry. Things sink very quickly even when it's a clear gravel bottom, like this. Get your face down to it, and search every square inch."

After the first night, Petrella's memories of that week became blurred. The work, during the hour that they stayed underwater, was not only monotonous, it was detached, trance-like and other-worldly. Their only interrupters were fish, attracted by the beam of the torch, who would swim up, lazy and fearless, to examine the new planet which had arisen in their watery hemisphere. One large carp Petrella got to know quite well. It would hang, hardly moving, in front of his face, dart provocatively away, and then slowly return. Petrella decided, in the end, that it was trying to make love to him.

At the conclusion of each lateral movement of the search he would meet Borden. They would work up to each other until his right hand touched Borden's left, then they would depart, silently, to the outer edge of the area, move forward the peg which marked their progress, and so start again.

At the end of the hour the cold drove them to the surface. They stripped their suits and pummelled some warmth back into each other's bodies. Then they dressed, made their way back to the car, and went home to bed. And to sleep. Petrella had to be up at six and it was, perhaps, this continued shortage of sleep that gave, in remembrance, such an air of unreality to that week.

He remembered the highlights. The moment when Super-intendent Haxtell walked into the CID room and told them that the Corinne Hart case was finished.

"Right or wrong," he said, "I decided to work on his mother. I persuaded her in the end that it wasn't really safe for her son to stay free. She's not only withdrawn her alibi, she's prepared to give evidence against him."

"Guilty but insane?"

"Diminished responsibility anyway," said Haxtell. (Kellaway had said, "Once the jury's out, I'm finished." That was Haxtell's view too. Like most policemen, he cared little what happened ultimately to his victims; unless they happened to have killed a policeman, in which case they ought to be hanged and he felt uneasy until this had happened.)

Then there were the visits, one a day, to Collins' shop, to study the postcards in the glass showcase; postcards which offered sewing machines and perambulators for sale, deep massage, and lodgings for lonely young men, but none of them seemed to carry any particular message for Petrella. He wondered if the whole incident of the white-faced girl might have been a hallucination. Something imagined between waking and sleeping.

It was on the fourth night, remembered for its cold, unrelenting rain, that they were startled, on returning to the car, by a cloaked figure which stepped out of the shadows and shone a torch upon them.

"Good evening."

"Good evening, Bateson," said Petrella.

"Oh, it's you, Sergeant."

"Who did you think it was, car thieves?"

"Didn't recognize the car," said Bateson. "I been keeping an eye on her for some time."

"Then you can take your eye off," said Petrella. "Because we're going home to bed. Good night."

"Will he tell anyone about us?" asked Borden, as they drove off.

"He won't tell anyone," said Petrella. "He'll simply put it in his occurrences book. It's sort of a personal log all policemen keep. 'Last night at 2 a.m. I observed Councilor Brassey returning to his house. I said good night to him. He said good night to me.'"

"Sounds a waste of time," said Borden.

"Surprisingly, it isn't. Did you know that the men who shot Antiquis in London were caught because a constable down at Southend made an entry in his occurrences book four days *before* the murder took place?"

Borden said, no, he didn't know that, and drove in thoughtful silence for a few minutes.

"Who sees that book?"

"His sergeant."

"It was a mistake ever teaching policemen to read."

It was on the following night, the fifth of their search, that Borden failed to reappear at the end of the dive. They had known before they started that there was a bare sixty minutes of pressure left in their aqualungs and they had slightly hastened the search to give themselves a safety margin.

Petrella was getting ready to go down and look for him, when the frogman's head broke surface. They paddled in silence to the bank.

"What kept you?" said Petrella. "I began to think you were in trouble."

"Just at the end of the square," said Borden, "right on the dead ball line, as you might say, I felt something. I'm sure of it. You can almost sense it, when the bottom's been churned up and settled down again. And there was a good deal of activity among our fishy hosts."

"Did you – ?"

"I hadn't time. I felt the air beginning to suck dry, so I came up quick. We'll finish this job tomorrow night, Patrick."

That was Monday night. It was on Tuesday morning that Kellaway sent for Petrella. He could read trouble in Dodds' face. It stood up, like a thick black ridge of thundercloud. The storm hit him as he entered the room.

Kellaway was standing. He was so angry that he was past all the ordinary signs of anger. He was a little whiter than usual but his voice was almost civil.

"Will you kindly explain," he said, "what the devil you're up to in that reservoir?"

Petrella did so, as best he could. His words fell into a pool of inky silence.

"And is this stunt something you're doing in your own time, to improve your health? Or is it connected with the Reservoir Case?"

There were dangers both ways. Petrella said, "It sort of arises out of the Reservoir Case."

"Then if it's police work, why has no report been put in?"

Why, indeed?

Kellaway said, "I warned you as nicely as I could, some days ago, to lay off this self-advertising stunt of yours. Just come out of the clouds for a moment. You're not Sexton Blake. You're a probationary detective sergeant in the Metropolitan Police Force and you're under my orders, which I thought were clear enough to be understood, even by you. I don't want to make an official matter out of this and put some mark on your book which will stop you getting promotion. But you step out of line once more, and that's what I'll have to do. Have I succeeded in making myself clear this time?"

"Yes, sir," said Petrella. "Quite clear."

"Have you got anything more you want to say about it?"

"No, sir."

"Then I've got one thing more. You've been called as a witness when the case opens at the Central Criminal Court, which looks like being tomorrow. A lot of your evidence was only formal, so I've arranged to dispense with it or do it some other way."

He paused, and added, "There's no sense in taking the field in a Cup Final, with a player who may shoot through his own goal."

11

Old Bailey - First Day's Play

Mr Justice Rowan looked like an actor of the modern school; the school begotten by Television out of Cinema, in which sincerity of manner and a good frontal bone structure were much more important than the classic profile.

Like most of Her Majesty's judges, he disliked hearing capital charges. They were, in his experience, an excuse for the intrusion of all sorts of sentiment, obscurantism, and theatricality into an occasion which should be logical and judicial.

He looked warily around him as the court rose at his entrance. Charles Younger, he saw, of senior Treasury counsel. And with him Margesson, the most brilliant and painstaking of the juniors. The Crown, he concluded, must have a shaky case if they had put two such stars together to open the batting.

For the defence, Claude Wainwright, a real old warhorse, noted in the popular press for his slashing attacks on the police, but give him a real point of law and he could argue it well enough. Only a fortnight ago, in the much-to-be-preferred atmosphere of Queen's Bench, he had listened for three days while Mr Wainwright had tried to persuade him that the holder of a bill of exchange endorsed generally had equal rights against both the original issuer and his transferee.

Mr Wainwright's junior, a man older even than Mr Wainwright, he was not conscious of having seen before.

The jury looked as baffled and inert as juries usually looked at the beginning of a heavy case. Probably they would come to life later. The public gallery was full and the press box grossly overcrowded. He had called attention to this before, but no one had done anything about it. One day they would get a really sensational case and a pressman would die of suffocation.

Peine forte et dure.

The preliminaries over, Mr Younger rose to his feet. He had thick, black hair, bright brown eyes, and a face like an intelligent prize fighter.

He said, "This is a case in which the Crown charges capital murder against the accused, Howton, for the killing, by shooting, on September 22nd last, at or near the Binford Park Reservoir, of Rosa Marion Ritchie, the wife of Alfred Ritchie, whose whereabouts are at the moment unknown, but who, at that date, himself had very recently escaped from one of Her Majesty's prisons, where he was being detained on a criminal charge."

Mr Younger looked at the jury for the first time and added, "I have stressed the position of the deceased woman's husband at this early stage in the proceedings because although absent – he is believed by the police to be in France – he plays an important part in this story. The view taken by the Crown is that this is what might perhaps be described as a gang killing: I can think of no more dignified words for an essentially sordid crime, committed in part at least for gain, by an associate of a known criminal."

Mr Younger was, here, on very delicate ground, and no one knew it better than himself. The sentence which he had just thrown, apparently impromptu, had cost him and his junior many anxious hours to compose.

"To understand the case properly, you must know that Ritchie was an active and successful larcenist. He headed a group which concentrated on robbing jewellers' shops. Not the very largest shops, in the West End, which are usually adequately protected, but somewhat smaller ones on the outskirts of the central districts and in the suburbs. It was a North London gang, and most of the offences took place in North London. At the time of Ritchie's arrest the police had compiled, and I shall produce to you, a long list of pieces, mostly small diamonds, gold and platinum, which they were thought to have taken. When Ritchie was arrested, more than a year ago, and his gang dispersed, very little of this jewellery was discovered. I shall try to show you that it had been placed in the hands of his wife who, on her own account or acting on his instructions, had hidden it.

"We now come to the first concrete fact, in this curious chain of facts, which it will be my duty to set before you. From the moment that Ritchie, the author of these thefts, disappeared behind bars, the proceeds of his crimes started to reappear, in bits and pieces, sometimes in altered form, on the market. We shall produce four witnesses who were offered, or have actually purchased, such jewellery. They are, I need hardly add, perfectly honest men, pawnbrokers and jewellers, and they have helped the police considerably in their inquiries. Two of these men definitely, and one less definitely, have identified the accused as the man who disposed of the jewels to them.

"I shall further show, by the testimony of the lady with whom the deceased lodged, a Mrs Fraser, that during the whole of the period between her husband going to prison and the supposed time of her death, Mrs Ritchie was" – Mr Younger paused delicately – "in touch with the accused, going out to meet him on three or four occasions that we know of, and very likely on other occasions as well.

"This, then, is the picture. This is what was happening during the first eight or nine months of last year. Matters were precipitated by an event which neither the accused nor Mrs Ritchie could well have foreseen. On September 21st last, Ritchie escaped on his way from a London prison to permanent detention. It is not known how he spent the first night of his freedom nor what happened to him thereafter, although there is secondary evidence, which I will produce to you for what it is worth, that he crossed to France and has remained there ever since.

"On the following day, Saturday, September 22nd, which is a date you will have to remember very carefully, Mrs Ritchie went to the grounds of the Binford Park Reservoir. We do not know at what time, except that she left her lodgings before three o'clock, and one of the minor mysteries of the case is how she managed to get into the grounds of the reservoir at all. But that she went there is past dispute, for she remained there, and there her body was found, under a covering of hastily scraped-up leaves, some six weeks later.

"The accused also went to the reservoir."

Mr Younger turned and looked at Howton, who stared sullenly back, single red eye ablink.

"Three people, local residents, have now been found by the police who saw him at it, or near it, that night. He was accompanied by certain – associates. One witness observed him climbing into the grounds of the reservoir itself. A tragedy might have been averted had she informed someone in authority of what she had seen, but since she was over seventy and alone in the house, you may feel that she is not greatly to be blamed.

"We are now in the realms of conjecture. I will give you the facts, as they are known to us, and you will have to draw your own conclusions from them. At some time – it is reasonable to suppose that it was that night, unless he was in the habit of visiting the reservoir regularly – the accused entered the small cottage at the southern end of the reservoir. We know that he was there because he left his fingerprints on the paintwork of the living-room window when he climbed in. The cottage was at that time standing empty, the employee of the Water Board who occupied it having departed. Another curious fact of this case is that, despite the efforts of the police, and in spite of the publicity which attended the earlier proceedings, this man, a Mr Ricketts, has not come forward. He may or may not have anything to do with the case, but one would have thought that he would have come forward to say, 'I am the man you are talking about.' One would have thought that he would have done this, if – "

An unbiased observer swears that Mr Younger paused for a full five seconds after the word "if". In the deep silence someone was heard to gasp. A quick drawing-in of breath. It was not the prisoner. He was staring fixedly ahead of him.

" – if only to assist the police in their inquiries," concluded Mr Younger mildly.

"The next fact to consider is that a boat, customarily kept at the foot of the cottage garden, was found, sunk and abandoned, at the opposite end of the reservoir and that, roughly halfway along its course, a diver, working for the police, recovered, from the bed of the reservoir, an automatic pistol. It was at a point too far from the shore for it to have been thrown. Tests have shown, quite conclusively, that it was from this gun, pressed up against her side, that the bullet was fired which killed Mrs Ritchie. Other witnesses will depose that they have seen the accused in possession of this gun or one very like it."

"That's a lie," said Howton.

"Silence," said the usher.

"It's a —ing lie, and the man who says it's a —ing liar."

"Mr Wainwright," said the judge, "will you explain to your client that he will have an opportunity of giving evidence himself if he wishes, at the proper time."

"If Charlie Garden says it's my gun, there's things I can tell you about Charlie Garden – "

Mr Wainwright arose, but not, it was remarked, with any undue speed, and said, "I much regret the irregular observations made by my client and agree that they ought to form no part of the record."

"Very well, Mr Younger," said the judge.

"At this stage," said Mr Younger, "I should add only a word about motive. I have indicated, in outline, what the Crown will try to show you, through its witnesses. It will bring Rosa Ritchie to the reservoir, and it will bring the accused to the reservoir, with a gun. And it will leave Rosa Ritchie dead, on the bank, with a bullet fired from that gun inside her; and the gun itself concealed, with some care, in the deepest part of the reservoir. And thereafter it will show you jewellery, formerly in the possession of the dead woman, being secretly disposed of by the accused. But there is necessarily a gap in the story. No one heard the shots. There was a silencer on the gun and it was pressed into the woman's side. No one has come forward who saw the murder committed. It would perhaps be surprising if they had. And no one knows with any certainty why the shot was fired. I could, of course, myself suggest a number of motives, and I have no doubt that your ingenuity could supply others. The matter is of secondary importance. His Lordship will, I know, guide you more fully on the relevant law in due course. At the moment all I need say is that there is no onus upon the prosecution to prove any motive at all. Many murders are committed without motive, or for motives so small as to be ludicrous."

"Murder without motive," scribbled the reporter from one of the brighter dailies. After a moment's thought he changed it to "apparently motiveless murder".

"I shall now call Dr Summerson, the pathologist who first examined the body."

Petrella spent the morning catching up with one or two routine jobs. After lunch he walked along to the Highside Infirmary, where he knew most of the sisters, having been assigned to guard the place a few months before when there had been attacks on nurses coming home after dark. The attacker had never been discovered, but Petrella had enjoyed his incursion into the curious, clean, cosy, regimented, adolescent life that went on behind the walls of that hideous Victorian structure.

Sister Macillroth received him in her sanctum. She said that Gover was still unconscious, but showing signs, at last, of returning animation.

"How on earth," said Petrella, "can he still be alive after all these days? I'd have thought lack of food – "

"Glucose injections."

"I see. Will he be likely to remember anything at all?"

"He won't sit bolt upright in his bed," said Sister Macillroth, "and give you a clear and conseestant account of just what took place."

"No. But will it ever come back?"

"Some of it will. Unless his brain's been affected pairmanently. But there'll always be a gap."

"How long?"

"Perhaps a few hours. Perhaps a day."

Petrella said, "Can I look at him?"

"It'll do him no harm that I can see."

They walked along noiseless corridors to the small room where Gover lay. A very pretty nurse, who had been sitting beside the bed, got up as they came in.

"He's moved again, twice," she said. "Once he rolled almost completely over."

Petrella peered down at Gover's face. It was very white. Even the lips were drained of colour, and the tight-shut lids were blue-veined.

"You'll send for us the moment he does come round, won't you?"

"Certainly not. The first person we shall send for will be the doctor, who will probably give him a drug to send him back to sleep again." She relented sufficiently to add, "We'll send for you second, Sergeant."

"Superintendent Kellaway," said Mr Wainwright, gathering his gown about him. "I have just a few questions to ask you. You have been in charge of the investigation into this case?"

"Yes."

"In place of, or assisting, the divisional detective staff?"

"In co-operation with them."

"But in charge of them."

"Yes."

"That is a somewhat unusual arrangement?"

"It is not, perhaps, very usual in the Metropolitan area, but quite common outside it."

"But Highside *is* in the Metropolitan area?"

"Certainly."

"Then I do not see the relevance of your answer."

Superintendent Kellaway said, without any trace of rancour, "I am sorry. My answer of course is that, being in the Metropolitan area, the arrangement *was* an unusual one."

He was well used to Mr Wainwright and knew that the first and the last rule was never to lose your temper.

"And what was there about this case that necessitated the introduction of eminent assistance from the central office?"

"Nothing at all."

"Then – ?"

"The whole arrangement was dictated by shortage of manpower in the division concerned."

"I see. At what time did you arrest the accused?"

"At what time?"

"That was my question. At what hour?"

"At approximately half past four in the morning."

"Indeed. And what made you select such a curious hour?"

"I wanted to make sure that he would be at home."

The ripple of laughter which this reply provoked was immediately suppressed by the ushers, but it did nothing to improve Mr Wainwright's temper.

"You were aware," he said, "of the address at which the accused was living?"

"Certainly."

"He was not in hiding? He was living there under his own name?"

"He hadn't advertised his presence there."

"Would you kindly answer my question?"

"Yes. So far as I know he was living there under his own name."

"Then you could have found him there at any time. Why did you select an hour of the morning more commonly associated with the activities of the Gestapo?"

(Considerable excitement in the press box. "QC attacks Police." " 'Gestapo methods,' says Wainwright.")

"I have explained before," said Kellaway, "that I should not have been certain, at any more orthodox hour, of finding him at home."

"I see. And after you had pulled him from his bed, in the middle of the night, and marched him down to the police station, what next transpired?"

"He was questioned."

"You interrogated him?"

"Yes."

"For how long?"

"I think we broke off for breakfast at about eight o'clock and were finished by midday."

Mr Wainwright made a show of counting on his fingers.

"Then am I right in saying that he was interrogated, practically without pause, for more than seven hours?"

"Well, there were pauses. To write down what he had said, and so on. It's a long business."

"It must have seemed so to the prisoner. How many inter-rogators were there?"

"I asked most of the questions. I was helped by Detective Sergeant Dodds, and Detective Constables Mote and Cobley took it in turns to write it down."

"Four of you," said Mr Wainwright, turning slightly toward the jury. "Four of you. For seven hours. Yes, I see – "

A black, thick darkness, broken only by the yellow light from the two helmet torches. Now that they had stopped searching and had started to dig, their lights were dimmed by the mud and sediment that their fingers were scrabbling up a few inches away from their faces.

They were living in a half world; a world in which sight and touch were effective, but ears and nose were cut off. All that Petrella could hear was a steady buzzing and throbbing inside his own head, caused by the exertion of the work which had set up all sorts of unexpected pressures inside his watertight shell. For a moment he felt the air sucking dry at the inlet, and panicked, and knew in the same instant that it was only imagination.

Their hands sank in deeper. It was there, right enough. Not a shadow of doubt. After five nights of patient searching, *this* was what they had come to find. It was bedded down and sunk into the soft mud and gravel but their efforts were stirring it. Shapeless, sodden, grotesque, inert, it was preparing to rise from its long sleep, up from the darkness of night and underwater, to the cruel light of day.

One complete arm was free now, one enormous flipper, the ends apparently encased in black leather. Then a leg, with a monstrous, padded thigh. Borden touched Petrella, and indicated that the time had come for them to lift. Both together. Hold it tight.

It was a little easier as the buoyancy of the water began to help them. Inch by inch they fought their way upward, hugged to the monster they were raising. Then the surface. Then the slow job of dragging shoreward the waterlogged hulk which rolled and surfaced and dipped and played in their wake.

As soon as they were ashore, Petrella stripped off his mask.

The charnel stench assaulted the sweet night. He stepped aside to control his heaving stomach.

Borden, impassive, stared down at their obscene salvage.

"They'll have to argue bloody hard," he said, "if they want to argue this one away."

12

Old Bailey – Final Day's Play

"Before opening the case for the defence," said Mr Wainwright, "I have a submission to make on a point of law."

"Yes, Mr Wainwright," said Mr Justice Rowan courteously. He had had a little bet with his clerk that Mr Wainwright would go for "no case". Well, Porter could afford to lose five shillings. Porter was a much richer man than he was.

"I would submit," said Mr Wainwright, "that there is no necessity for the defence to put forward its case at all. It is one of the fundamentals of the English legal system that the Crown must make out its case. The Crown must show that the accused murdered Rosa Ritchie by shooting her on September 22nd at Binford Park Reservoir. Not that he was *at* the reservoir. Even if that were admitted – and it is far from being admitted – it is a fairly long step to take from saying that a man was *at* a place to saying that he committed a murder there. All the evidence as to the murder is circumstantial. I hasten to add – and I say this because I am certain his Lordship will say it if I do not – that there are crimes which have to be proved by circumstantial evidence because no other sort is available. But" – Mr Wainwright turned round and glared for a moment at Mr Younger, sitting impassively beside him – "there is circumstantial evidence *and* circumstantial evidence, and my learned friend will perhaps excuse me if I say that the evidence he has seen fit to produce is circumstantial to the point almost of non-existence.

"He was good enough to point out that no cogent motive exists. A number of motives have been put forward. Indeed, so many that they must have reminded the jury of the famous clock that struck thirteen, the last note being not only absurd in itself but casting considerable doubt on the twelve that had gone before.

"The only direct link in the whole story which has been suggested between the dead woman and the accused, is the gun. And observe how weak that link is. I should like to emphasize. It is not denied that this is the gun which fired the bullet which killed Mrs Ritchie. All the weighty scientific evidence bearing on this point can be accepted – and put on one side. What is left? Two persons who say that they *think* they once saw the accused carrying a gun *like* the gun recovered from the water. That is the link which we are asked to believe will be strong enough to hang this man.

"I would say two things about it. First, that the pistol, as we have heard, is of a standard type, the *P*38 issued to the German Army, and issued by the hundred thousand. How many misguided souvenir hunters brought them back to England at the end of the last war I should not like to begin to calculate.

"The second point is that the witnesses who have, somewhat hesitantly, identified the pistol are neither of them worthy of a moment's credence in this Court. Both of them, as they admitted under my cross-examination, are professional criminals with long records of offences. Men who live by their wits, under the eye of the police, and who are only too willing, I imagine, to oblige those authorities under whose sufferance they live."

("QC again attacks Police. Were Witnesses Influenced?" scribbled the *Daily Courier* gleefully. It had got its knife into Scotland Yard ever since a scoop which one of its enterprising crime reporters had secured had been killed by the Yard's press relations officer.)

Mr Justice Rowan thought to himself that it must have been a terribly difficult decision to make. Clearly they were two vital witnesses, and if their credibility could be attacked, it should be.

They had, in fact, left a very poor impression on His Lordship. Nevertheless, by attacking them, counsel had opened a very dangerous sluice gate. For the rule of evidence, which, like most English legal rules, was based on rough notions of fair play, laid it down that a prisoner's own character and record could be attacked if he, in turn, saw fit to attack the character of the prosecution witnesses. "Those in glass houses – " as the old rule said. And the judge already knew (although it was to be hoped the jury did not) that in this sort of mud-slinging the prisoner would certainly come out second-best.

The alternative, of course, was not to allow the prisoner to give evidence at all. He looked a surly brute and would probably, although you could never tell, be a bad witness, one who would prejudice the jury against himself the moment he opened his mouth. And yet – not to give evidence at all! To offer no explanation of what did take place that night! It would be an exceedingly risky course and one calculated to annoy the jury even more than telling them some sort of story which they might believe or not. What perilous alternatives faced any advocate charged with the defence in a capital case. No one, except possibly a surgeon, had a life more exactly balanced upon his professional skill.

"I should therefore submit," concluded Mr Wainwright, "with confidence, that the defence has no case to answer."

The judge said, "The court is much obliged to you for your cogent presentation of this point. It must be ruled, however, as a matter of law, that the Crown has made out a case which requires answering."

"In this case," said Mr Wainwright, rising to his feet with renewed energy, "I will call the prisoner."

"In the name of heaven," said Superintendent Haxtell, who had been aroused at a godless hour from the first deep and satis-factory night's rest he had enjoyed since the discovery of Corinne Hart, and was, by now, in a brittle temper, "in the name of heaven, why didn't you tell someone what you were up to?"

"Well, sir – "

"You're a policeman, a member of a police force. You're quite entitled to have bright ideas, but when you have them, why not tell someone else about them and get them worked out properly?"

"I did tell someone. I told Kellaway that I was sure there was something else there."

"And what did he say?"

"He told me to leave it alone."

"Then why didn't you?"

This was an awkward one. Petrella was saved by the telephone bell. It was Dr Summerson.

"I've finished the autopsy," he said. "I gathered from your young man when he called me at four o'clock this morning that you might want the results in a hurry."

Haxtell said, "Hmp."

"Very interesting, medically. The body had been weighted with three heavy pieces of marble fender, inside the clothes, and it went straight down into the silt and stayed there. There's no current in a reservoir to knock it about, so it was in pretty good shape. I've sent the hands down to your laboratory."

"Will they get any prints?"

"No difficulty at all, I should say. The skin's pretty well intact. Particularly the right hand, which was under the body. This one was shot, too."

"You surprise me," said Haxtell bitterly.

"And has been dead, as far as one can tell, about the same length of time."

"Any chance of an identification – apart from fingerprints?"

"Face and general appearance, you mean? No. Not a chance of that. I noticed an old dislocation of the hip. It might have made the man hobble a bit, or it might not. Difficult to say. Failing the prints, the best thing would be to wait till they've got the clothes dried and sorted out and try someone on them. I may have some more for you later."

Haxtell thanked him, and dialled the Water Board. He caught Mr Lundgren at his desk. The General Manager said, "Another one? How – no one told me you were still working at the reservoir."

Haxtell passed that one up. He said, "What I wanted to find out was whether your man Ricketts had ever had a dislocated hip. It might have shown as a very slight limp."

"I'll look up his medical sheet," said Lundgren. "But I doubt if it'd show a thing like that. He was wounded, as a very young soldier, in the first war. Do you think – ?"

"I'm afraid so, yes," said Haxtell. "He never got to Blackpool. He got in the way of whatever was going on that night. We may need you, later on, to look at his clothes."

Lundgren said he would do what he could. Time was going on. It was eleven o'clock. Haxtell said, "There's one thing we must do. Tell Kellaway what's happened, and get the news down to the court. I don't know that it's going to make a lot of difference, but – "

Heavy steps in the corridor heralded the arrival of Chief Superintendent Barstow. He came through the door like a rhinoceros through a bamboo screen, turned a deeper shade of red when he saw Petrella, and jerked his head at him. Petrella removed himself.

Lurking nervously in the CID room he heard, muted by the intervening passages, the turbulent bass of Barstow in eruption, with shorter, softer passages from Haxtell's tenor. It was a performance which, at any other time, might have seemed amusing, but he felt no desire to laugh. He knew well enough that it was his bones they were fighting over.

"I think a certain amount of the blame must attach to Kellaway," Haxtell was saying. "I've noticed it before with these Central Office types. They think the rules don't apply to them. Surely, if there was a decision on policy to be taken – whether or not to carry on with the search after they found the gun – they should have referred it to you."

"Certainly," said Barstow. It had not, in fact, occurred to him before, but the point was one well calculated to appeal to him.

"I'm not prejudging the question of whether or not the search should have been widened. If it had been put to me – "

"If it had been put to *me*," said Barstow, "I should have said, never leave a job half done. But the point is, that it wasn't put to me."

"Kellaway is probably so used to being called in by doddering old chief constables, and taking complete charge, and running their shows for them, that it didn't occur to him that while he was in a London district – "

"Exactly," said Barstow.

"I'm not saying it wasn't wrong of Sergeant Petrella to do what he did."

"Absolutely irregular."

"And if a disciplinary complaint has been made – "

"We must deal with that when it arises. The first thing is to get this news down to Kellaway."

"We tried his house as soon as we knew what it was all about, but he had gone. We tried the court too, but he hadn't turned up there."

"He could hardly leave court until the summing-up's over," said Barstow. "Try them again."

"So you never went to the Binford Park Reservoir," said Mr Younger.

"That's right," said Howton.

"Neither on that night nor any other night."

"That's right."

"And if you never went to the reservoir, of course, you never went to the reservoir cottage."

"That's right."

"Then how would you account for the fact that a full set of the prints of your right hand were found in the paint work of the cottage window?"

"*If* they were found there."

"I'm afraid I don't quite follow that answer."

"It's only the police say they found them."

"I see. You are suggesting that the whole of that evidence was faked by the police."

"That's right."

"The jury will have to decide for themselves on the value of that suggestion," said Mr Younger politely. "Are you the owner of a blue Riley saloon car, registration number GKR692?"

"No."

"Have you ever owned such a car?"

"No."

"Have you ever hired, or used, such a car?"

"Yes. I hired one."

"And you were using it in September last?"

"As far as I can remember."

"And, as you have heard, one of the witnesses, a Mrs Gurney, observed a car with this number drive up to the reservoir and a man whom she has identified as you, and the other men, who correspond closely in description to friends of yours, get out of it."

"I heard her say so."

"You mean that she made it up?"

"I mean, if she saw someone, it wasn't me."

"Then she made a mistake."

"That's right."

"And she imagined the number of the car."

"That's right."

"A curious coincidence that she should have imagined a number that exactly corresponded to the number of your car."

"Of course it wasn't a coincidence," said Howton. "The police told her what number to say."

"I see. The whole of this evidence is also an invention of the police."

"That's right."

"And the evidence of Mr Carver and Miss Brownlow?" (Mr Carver and Miss Brownlow were a courting couple unearthed by the efforts of Sergeant Dodds.) "Who saw you returning to your parked car just before midnight. And were so suspicious of your behaviour that they, also, took a note of the number?"

"I don't believe they saw anything."

"Then where would you suggest they got their information from?"

"I don't know. They read it in the papers, perhaps."

"As far as I am aware, no mention of your name ever appeared in the papers."

"Then someone told them."

"Told them what?"

"Told them," said Howton, "that the police were after pinning the killing onto me. There's some sort of people, as soon as they hear that, they'll come forward and say anything."

(Why anyone should have imagined, thought Mr Justice Rowan, that it was in the interests of the prisoner that he should be allowed to give evidence passed the bounds of human understanding.)

"Come again," said Petrella, into the telephone. "You've got what? Damn this line. I'm sorry, I can't hear you. No, that's better."

"Sergeant Blinder. Fingerprints here," said the voice patiently. "I want to speak to Sergeant Petrella."

"You're speaking to him."

"Oh, it's you, is it, Patrick. Look here, I've got an identification for you."

"Of those prints we sent you this morning? That's quick work."

"Not those. They're still working on them."

"What are you talking about, then?"

"A single print you submitted about a week ago."

"That," said Petrella. He had forgotten all about it. "Who – ?"

"It's not an absolutely firm identification, mind you. It wasn't a complete print."

"I think it's marvellous that you should have got anything out of it at all."

"It's a man called Bancroft."

The name meant nothing to Petrella.

"I found it in the Aged File. The man was a soldier. Age given on the card as eighteen. It was a charge of assault and robbery, but apparently the robbery was dropped, and it was heard as simple assault. I'd guess he was on leave on a spree, or something."

"What year was all this?"

"1918."

"1918!" said Petrella. "You're sure it wasn't 1818?"

"The science of fingerprinting had not been developed in 1818," said Sergeant Blinder coldly. "I'll send the details round in the course of the morning."

Petrella passed this on to Superintendent Haxtell who was in the middle of a third unsuccessful attempt to get hold of Kellaway. He said, "I don't think there's much point in passing this little titbit on to the DPP until we know a little more about it. When are we going to get it?"

"Blinder said, in the course of the morning."

"Which probably means teatime," said Haxtell. "Hullo, what's this?"

His office window commanded the courtyard where the police cars stood. A police cadet motorcyclist was propping his machine up. He had a large brown envelope in his hand.

"Something tells me," said Haxtell, "that this is it."

Petrella ran down the stairs, collected the envelope, signed for it, and came back with it.

"Quick work, for once," he said. "Now perhaps we shall find out something about Mr Bancroft. Do you suppose – "

He broke off.

Superintendent Haxtell was staring at the contents of the envelope in complete silence. From where he stood Petrella could see two photographs, and clipped to them a memorandum sheet, headed Fingerprint Section, New Scotland Yard, and covered with typescript.

Haxtell finished reading the memorandum; turned it over to see if there was anything further on the back, and then parcelled it up with the photographs and put it slowly back in the envelope. Not until then did he say, "This is nothing to do with the gun. This is the report on the man you pulled out of the reservoir last night."

"I recalled you, Superintendent," said the judge, "because I wanted you to assist me, and the jury, over one small point which has not emerged quite clearly from the evidence."

"I'll do what I can, my Lord."

"I'm sure you will. It is this cottage. The reservoir cottage, it is called. As I understand the matter, in the ordinary way it would be occupied by an employee of the Metropolitan Water Board."

"That is so."

"And had been so occupied up to the supposed day of the murder."

"I think the last time anyone actually saw him, my Lord, was the afternoon before."

The judge studied his notes carefully, and said, "I think you are right. The Water Board foreman, Mr Stokes, when giving evidence, said that he had spoken to Ricketts the night before. But what I wanted to know was this: did the police attach any particular significance to the coincidence that Ricketts should have walked out of his cottage on the day of – or possibly the day before – the killing of Mrs Ritchie?"

"We thought about it a good deal, my Lord. But we did not, in the end, conclude that there was any connection between the two events."

"There is no reason why they should be connected," agreed the judge. "I take it that efforts were made to get hold of Ricketts?"

"Certainly."

"And he has not come forward? Even though the case has now received considerable publicity."

"To the best of my knowledge, my Lord, Ricketts has not come forward at all. Certainly he has made no effort to contact the police – "

"I'm afraid," said the man on the telephone courteously, "that no one can speak to Superintendent Kellaway just at this moment. He is in the witness box."

"In the witness box?"

'The judge asked for him to be recalled. He had some questions to put to him before he commenced summing up."

"I see. Could a message be got to him, just as soon as he's out of the box, that Chief Superintendent Barstow and Superintendent Haxtell want to see him urgently. They are on their way down to the court now."

"Chief Superintendent Barstow and Superintendent Haxtell. Very good, sir. I'll see if I can get a message to him as soon as he's free."

"It's most important."

"I got the first half of your message all right," said Kellaway. "Jumped straight into a car and went back to Crown Road. When I got there, they told me you were down at the court. So I came straight back again. We must have passed each other on the way. I gather, incidentally, that Sergeant Petrella has been putting in some more overtime."

He didn't say it angrily. There was a cool undertone of amusement in his voice.

"Yes," said Barstow. He, too, was being unusually restrained. The situation was pregnant with difficulty, and at this stage probably the less said the better.

"I gather he's found Ricketts," said Kellaway. "I don't suppose it would have made much difference to this case, except as confirmatory evidence. I have always had it in mind that Ricketts may have got in the way of Howton that night, and stopped the second bullet – and been dumped along with the gun."

"No doubt," said Barstow. "Only it wasn't Ricketts he found. It was Monk Ritchie."

Kellaway stared at him.

"That's right. A perfectly clear identification of both hands. No doubt about it at all."

The door opened quietly and a uniformed attendant looked in.

"The jury are back, gentlemen," he said. "Guilty. His Lordship is pronouncing sentence now."

13

À la Recherche du Temps Perdu

"I've been forty years in the Metropolitan Police Force," said Barstow, "and I can't remember anything like it."

"It's a pretty good tangle," agreed Haxtell.

They were in Haxtell's office at Crown Road. A week had gone by since a jury had found Howton guilty of capital murder and Mr Justice Rowan had pronounced sentence of death on him; an event which had attracted the routine amount of press comment and the routine protests, but no more. Even the most ardent opponents of capital punishment had not felt Boot Howton to be a very promising martyr.

"The story about us finding the second body got into the local papers," said Haxtell. "Somebody saw the ambulance driving away with it and put two and two together. Naturally they all jumped to the conclusion that it was Ricketts who had been found. And we haven't taken any steps to undeceive them, yet."

"They weren't the only people who thought it was Ricketts," said Barstow.

"No, indeed."

"I suppose there's no doubt about *that.*"

"Of all the facts in this case, sir," said Haxtell, "that seems to be one of the few stone-cold certainties. The fingerprints alone, of course, were conclusive."

Barstow said, "There have been moments in this case when my belief in the infallibility of our fingerprint system has been rudely shaken. But go on."

"Even without the prints there was quite enough secondary evidence for a normal identification. The medical and dental particulars from the prison records all tallied. He was even wearing his prison underclothes, with his prison number on them. And now we have the Reverend Platt."

"Who the devil is he?"

"The Reverend Platt came into a small legacy last summer and decided to broaden his mind by continental travel. He found it very much to his taste, and returned regretfully to this country on Christmas Day, that being the last day for which his return ticket was valid. Several weeks later it occurred to British Railways that there had been an inquiry about this particular ticket, so they got hold of me, and I called on the Reverend Platt. In a sort of way he doesn't look unlike Monk Ritchie. I can quite see how the mistake arose. A clergyman, in mufti, out to enjoy his first continental holiday would tend to look rather like an escaping criminal, don't you think?"

Barstow grunted. In his view, the whole case was a deplorable shambles, and a warning against inviting the interference of the Central Authority into district matters. However, there was a point of procedure which had to be cleared up.

He said, "I've seen the DPP's office. As far as I could understand the young gentleman in striped trousers that I spoke to – and who sounded as if he'd got a hot potato in his mouth – they're supremely uninterested in Monk Ritchie. They're assuming that Howton shot him, too, which, of course, he may have done. And since Howton's been nicely convicted for the first killing, why should they lose any sleep over the second one?"

"Except, of course – "

"Thank you, I can see the feebleness of that point of view perfectly well myself. However, two can play at that game. If they're sticking to the book, I'm sticking to the book too. A dead man's been found, in my manor. No one's been charged yet with his death. Therefore it's my job to carry out an investigation. Right?"

"Right," said Haxtell. There were rare moments when he found Barstow refreshing, and this was one of them.

"I'm putting you in charge. We won't assume that this case is anything to do with the other killing. In fact, we won't assume any damn thing at all."

"Splendid," said Haxtell. "I suppose, as it's an ordinary routine investigation, there's no reason I shouldn't use Sergeant Petrella on it."

"Ah," said Barstow. "Petrella."

There was an unhappy pause.

"Yes," said Barstow again. "Petrella."

He swallowed deeply. The air was heavy with unanswered questions.

Then he said, "It would certainly be sensible to use him. He knows more about the background than anyone else. The blasted young idiot."

"Did Kellaway insist on his pound of flesh?"

"He put in a report, yes. Direct refusal to obey orders. I've seen a copy. It's quite fair as far as it goes. There's bound to be a disciplinary board. They can't overlook it."

"When it comes to the point," said Haxtell grimly, "I should like to put in a report too."

"If you do," said Barstow, "I shall tear it up. We've had too many damned reports and notes and minutes altogether. What do you think we are? The Civil Service? What you've got to do is get on and sort this mess out. Use Petrella as much as you like, and anyone else you like, and let's stop behaving like a lot of bloody old women."

"That suits me," said Haxtell.

As soon as Barstow had stumped off, Haxtell sent for Petrella. He gave him an edited version of what had occurred.

"One thing's quite clear," he said. "We've got to find Ricketts. And so far there's only one place we know he *isn't*. That's in the reservoir."

This was quite true. The reservoir had now been officially searched from end to end, and side to side, and so thoroughly that a bent sixpence could hardly have escaped notice.

"We've got to set about this logically. First, let's assume that Ricketts had nothing to do with the killing and see where that gets us. It would mean that he had strong, but private, reasons for clearing out. And that it was a fluke that he happened to clear out that day. If that's right, then it was Howton who took the boat out, and dumped Ritchie and the gun."

"Having weighted Ritchie down with three pieces of marble fender which we now find came *from the cottage.*"

"Yes. But we know Howton was in the cottage, anyway. The prints on the window show that."

"We don't know *why* he was in the cottage."

"Well – presumably it was his base of operations."

"If he was working from the cottage, why didn't he bring the boat back and put it quietly away where he found it?"

"There are plenty of loose ends," agreed Haxtell. "But let's go on with it and see where it takes us. *If* Ricketts had nothing to do with it, where is he now? From all accounts he was an independent, solitary sort of man. No family ties. Went where he liked, did what he liked."

"He was a rolling stone, all right," agreed Petrella.

"Then there's nothing impossible in the idea that he's rolled off somewhere and is living quietly under another name. As long as we don't bother him, he's not going to put himself forward. Particularly in a messy sort of murder case."

Petrella thought about it. Then he said, "It sounds all right, but I don't believe a word of it."

"I'm not sure that I believe it myself. But what's the alternative?"

"The alternative," said Petrella, "is that Ricketts shot both Rosa and Monk."

"Yes. And why?"

"I haven't any idea," said Petrella. "Perhaps they were disturbing the swans. Anyway, he leaves Rosa where she is, being fairly happy that she won't be found. And dumps Monk in the deepest part of the reservoir, along with the gun he used for the killings."

"Which was a souvenir he'd had from his army days. That's why it was so deep in grease."

"Right. And – " concluded Petrella triumphantly, "he couldn't go back to the cottage and the landing stage, because by that time *Howton and the boys were in possession.*"

They looked at each other.

"It's got possibilities," agreed Haxtell. "We still want a lot of answers. If it's right, then the print on the gun *must* be Ricketts'. It couldn't be anyone else. Only it appears to belong to a character called Bancroft, who got into trouble, once and once only, when on leave from the army in the First World War."

"Ricketts was just old enough to be in that war. Lundgren said so. He said he lied about his age to get in. That would make him – what? Seventeen in the last year of that war. And in his late fifties now."

"Which ties up all right with our man."

"So all we've got to do is to prove that Bancroft is Ricketts and we're home and dry."

"We've got to do a lot more than that," said Haxtell. "We've got to show some connection between Bancroft, Ricketts and the Howtons and the Ritchies." He thought for a moment. "This seems to split itself up into two jobs, doesn't it? Suppose I get Mote onto the Bancroft end. He can start down at the Fingerprint Section. Get what details they can give him there, and work his way forward. You tackle the Ricketts side. See Lundgren again. He'll know the name of Ricketts' army pals. Work through them. And don't waste any time. You've got a deadline of eight days."

Petrella stared at him.

Haxtell said, "Howton's case comes up before the Court of Criminal Appeal tomorrow week. I've just heard. It's been expedited."

Detective Constable Mote, whose hobby of photography has already been mentioned, was a conscientious young cockney

141

with curly hair, who had come to the police via the lower deck of the Royal Navy. He was a painstaking performer, and this was as well, for there was tribulation in store for him.

"I can't tell you anything more about this print than I have done," said Sergeant Blinder, when appealed to. "It seems to me everyone's making a lot too much of it. If you'll look at my report again you'll see what I said." He ran a finger down the typescript. " 'Much distorted.' Well, you couldn't expect anything else from a fingerprint made in mineral jelly. Mineral jelly's not plaster of Paris, you know."

Mote agreed that mineral jelly wasn't plaster of Paris.

"If you ask me, it's a miracle we picked it up at all. If anyone had told me a fingerprint could go underwater and come up six weeks later almost as good as new, I'd have called him a liar."

Mote said that the whole thing reflected the greatest possible credit on the efficiency and technical skill of the Fingerprint Section and on Sergeant Blinder in particular.

"Mind you," said Sergeant Blinder. "There's five points of similarity between this print and the second, and I'd say that was quite enough to work on, particularly when one of them's a reversed delta with a double inlet. But I couldn't get up in court and swear to it. You want eight points or more for the court."

Mote agreed that eight points were better than five. In common with most policemen, he understood very little about the niceties of fingerprint classification, having found the lectures on it boring. All that he really wanted was the details from the record and these, after ten minutes' further mollification of Sergeant Blinder, he got.

In faded ink, on the yellowing form, he read the recorded particulars of Robert Lowry Bancroft who, forty years before, had stumbled into the path of the law. Age eighteen. Height five foot eight inches. Occupation, Armed Forces (Infantry). (They might at least have given his regiment, thought Mote.) Peculiarities and distinguishing marks, Nil. (Naturally!) Previous convictions, Nil. Aliases, Nil. And an address at 14 Culver Street, Battersea.

"And you can bet your bottom dollar," said Mote, "that Culver Street's been pulled down and a ruddy great block of flats put up." It was one of those days.

Culver Street was still there. It looked as if it had been there forever. The bricks, red and yellow in their springtime, were now a deep and desperate black. The front gardens had merged into forecourts, and had then been trampled into the street itself. The occupants of No. 14 had been there since 1948. They knew nothing of the people who had had the house before them except that they had been "evacuated". This was the word which greeted Mote at every turn. Evacuation. There had been a break, a severing of the historic development of the street, sharp and decisive as a landslip. The little families had been bundled out. Few had come back again.

Mote found one old lady whose memory went back beyond two wars. She remembered the Mafeking Day celebrations. But she remembered no Bancrofts.

Those tried friends of authority, the Housing Department, the Church, and the Labour Exchange, had nothing to offer. They, too, spoke of the evacuation, and of their records which had been destroyed in the blitz. Mote called it a day and went home.

The next day he tried the War Office. When they understood what he wanted they packed him off down to Staines where, in a disused motor-car factory, lay stored the documentary records of the British Army's past.

"1918," said the sergeant major clerk. "Why, certainly. We go back a lot further than that. What unit are you looking for?"

"Not a unit. A man."

"And you don't know what regiment he was in?"

"I'm afraid not. Just that he was in the infantry."

"And all you know about him is his name?"

"That's right."

"Well, it's going to be a bit of a job, isn't it?"

He led him along corridors, through transepts, down further corridors, all lined, above head height, with slatted racks, and, on the racks, boxes and boxes of paper. There were millions of them. Hundreds of thousands of millions of them.

"Haven't you got some sort of index?" he said.

At this suggestion, the sergeant major clerk laughed, so loud that he roused a family of bats, which swooped across angrily, casting great shadows under the naked overhead lights.

Petrella, too, was encountering difficulties. He had found Lundgren in an unco-operative mood.

"I wish I'd never let you into my reservoir," he said. "It's been nothing but trouble."

"I'm sure they've finished now."

"I should hope so too. They wouldn't like me to drain it for them, perhaps?"

"No. I'm sure that won't be necessary."

After a time, he unbent so far as to admit that it probably wasn't Petrella's fault personally. But he hoped there wasn't going to be any further bother. The Board were getting restive.

"This is nothing to do with the Metropolitan Water Board," said Petrella. "It's a bit of ancient history. I want to find out everything I can about Ricketts personally."

"I'm surprised he hasn't been in touch with you. I should have thought he would have been bound to have read it all in the papers."

"That's what we thought too."

"And yet I don't know that I am so surprised. Ricketts was an odd sort of chap. Superficially very friendly, but I doubt if he had any real friends. He was a good deal older than the ordinary run of chaps in the battery. When he went out he usually went alone."

"A self-contained sort of person," suggested Petrella.

"That's right."

"Do you think he might have had some sort of past?"

Lundgren reflected. "It's easy to imagine things like that, after the event," he said. "But now that you put it to me, I shouldn't be entirely surprised. I don't necessarily mean anything criminal.

144

I mean that one just got the impression that he was a bit of a man of mystery."

"Was he married?"

"I think he drew a marriage allowance. Although that's not always the same thing. I'd have said, he was the sort of man who was quite attractive to a certain sort of woman. You know how they go for the quiet, grey-haired, fatherly type."

"Yes," said Petrella. He found a very different picture building up in his mind from the rough Water Board labourer he had started by visualizing.

"Army records should be able to give you some information about that. I'm sorry I haven't been able to help you more."

"On the contrary," said Petrella.

This time the War Office were able to be more helpful. Their 1939–45 records were in good order and, given proper particulars, they turned up Ricketts' paybook and identity documents without trouble.

Petrella ran his eye down the page. There was something there that might be useful. Next of kin. "Wife. Dorothy Mabel Ricketts, Forge Cottage, Bearsted, Kent."

"That would only be a wartime address, I expect," said the officer in charge of records. "She was probably evacuated there."

"Never mind," said Petrella, "it's a start."

He took the afternoon train from Victoria to Maidstone, and a local train brought him to the pleasant Kentish village of Bearsted, which huddles round a green where cricket is still played in the summer and the dogs and children from the nice houses nearby chase each other all the year round. Forge Cottage stood in a side turning, south of the green. It was a quiet, clap-boarded affair buried up to the neck in a garden which had spilled over onto the roadway.

The woman who opened the door to him was, he guessed, about fifty; thickset, grey-haired, and unsmiling.

Petrella introduced himself.

"It's a long time ago," he said apologetically. "Someone who may have been evacuated here during the war. A Mrs Ricketts."

"You'd better come in," she said, and called out, "Mother."

An old lady in black appeared from an inner room. "It's a gentleman from the police, Mother. He's asking for Mrs Ricketts."

They both stared at him, and Petrella felt uncomfortable under this convergent gaze.

"If you have any information – " he said.

"I'm Mrs Ricketts," said the grey-haired woman. "I'll tell you anything I can, but if it's my husband you're looking for, I warn you, it won't be much, for I haven't set eyes on him for more than twenty years."

"Another dead end," said Petrella. "She was as helpful as she could be but it didn't amount to much. They got married in 1924. When she was eighteen. They never had any children. He was away from home a lot, and pretty soon she began to think he'd set up a second home of his own somewhere."

Haxtell looked up sharply, and Petrella said, "Yes. That's the type that seems to be emerging. It makes you wonder, doesn't it? By the time war broke out in 1939, she hadn't seen Sydney – that's his name, apparently – for two or three years. He'd been sending her a little money from time to time. She was back with her mum. When he joined the army he put her down as his wife and next of kin and the marriage allowance went to her. He had to do that. She'd have gone up to the War Office and raised hell if he hadn't. She knew her rights."

"And when the war was over – ?"

"As soon as he was out of the army, the money stopped."

"Didn't she do anything about that? He was still her husband."

"I asked her that," said Petrella. "And she said, 'I'd got a job and I didn't need the money. But to tell you the truth I was glad to see him go. He wasn't really a good man.' "

"She said that?"

"As near as I can remember it."

"She might have been right, at that," said Haxtell. "Where do we look next? Time's getting short."

It was on his way home that night that Petrella saw the card. He had given up visiting Collins' shop, having drawn a blank there so often. But since he had to go past it he stopped to look.

"The person," said the card, "who was asking about a job at the reservoir. Inquire within."

14

Jean Speaks Up

The little shop was lit by one economical bulb, and smelled like the inside of an empty biscuit tin. Petrella waited, then shuffled his feet, then coughed; none of this having any effect he took a half-crown out of his pocket and rapped it sharply on the wooden counter.

At this magical sound an inner door flew open and an old woman looked out.

"We're shut," she said. "I ought to have locked the door."

"I'm not a cash customer," said Petrella. "I came about one of your advertisements."

"It's my husband does them. He's at the doctor's. The time you have to waste at the doctor's since they came on the rates, it's a disgrace. In the old days you had to pay for 'em, but they were there when you wanted 'em."

Petrella picked the card out of the window and showed it to the old woman, who read it disinterestedly.

"I can't make head or tail of 'em," she said. "My husband does them."

"When'll he be back?"

"Might be hours, yet. You'd better come back tomorrow. I've known him sit in that waiting-room till eight o'clock. All those people, sitting in a room together, with different illnesses. It's not right. No wonder people catch things."

"I expect that's why the doctors do it," said Petrella. "To make more work for themselves."

The old woman looked at him suspiciously.

"But as it happens, this is rather urgent. So I'll come back in an hour's time."

The old woman had opened her mouth to protest when she was saved the trouble by the return of her husband.

"Got away quicker this time," he said. "Nothing but wind, Dr Maddison said. I wonder. It didn't feel like wind to me. What can I do for you, sir? We're shut."

"I came about this."

"Oh, yes."

"Well, here I am," said Petrella patiently. "It says 'Inquire within'. I'm inquiring."

"The party that left this card," said the man, "was most particular that her message should only be given to a – dang it, but I've gone and forgotten it – a foreign name."

"Petrella."

"Right. A Detective Sergeant Petrella."

Petrella produced his warrant card, which the man examined carefully.

"All right," he said. "That looks all right. You're to go to Flat 5, Number 74 Parsons Road – that's off Westbourne Grove. You know it?"

"I can find it. When do I go?"

"Any evening this week between six and seven, the lady said. She'd be there, if you wanted to talk to her. Come to think of it, that was Monday, and it's Thursday now, and nearly ten to seven, so it looks as if you'll have to wait till tomorrow."

"I told him he'd better wait till tomorrow," said the old lady.

Next morning there was an unexpected message for Petrella. It was from Messrs Carver, Harrowing and Livermore of Lincoln's Inn.

"Solicitors," said Gwilliam, who had taken the message. "An old aunt's died, I wooden be surprised, and left you a packet."

"The only old aunt I've got's ten years younger than I am," said Petrella, and dialled the number he had been given.

He was put through to Mr Harrowing, who introduced himself.

"I saw you in the Magistrate's Court," he said. "I don't think you were at the Old Bailey, were you? We're instructed on behalf of the prisoner."

"Oh, yes," said Petrella cautiously. He remembered, now, where he had seen the name.

"We wondered if you could come down and have a word with us. Or we'll come up and see you, if that's more convenient. There's a certain amount of urgency. The appeal in this matter comes on next Thursday."

"Well," said Petrella, "I'll have to find out if it's all right."

"I don't see why your bosses should make any difficulty about it," said Mr Harrowing. "After all, presumably we're both interested in the same thing, and that's to get at the truth."

"That's right," said Petrella. "All the same, I think I'd better check up. I'll ring you back."

"I can't say I like the idea," said Haxtell, when it was put to him, "but if you're going at all you'd better go willingly. They could subpoena you if they really wanted to."

"But why me? All they can know about me is that I gave evidence on one or two fairly unimportant points in the Magistrate's Court."

"And *didn't* give evidence at the Old Bailey."

"Yes. He mentioned that. You don't suppose – "

"I don't know," said Haxtell. "The thing to do is to go and find out what they're after. You needn't commit yourself. You can always pass the buck by saying that you have to refer to higher authority."

"What I really don't want is for anyone to think that I've been running off on my own bat, proffering information to the defence. I wouldn't – "

"No," said Haxtell, looking at him curiously. "No. That's all right. I don't think anyone thinks that. And by the way, I didn't tell you. Mote found Bancroft."

"He *what?*"

"I don't mean he found him in person. I mean he traced his 1914–18 record, or what was still left of it. Here's a copy."

He pushed a typewritten flimsy across the table and Petrella read:

"*Robert Lowry Bancroft.* Enlisted, January 1918. Age at enlistment, 18. Passed fit for General Service. France, May 1918. Posted 9th Royal South London Regiment. Acting Lance Corporal, July 1918. Rank confirmed August 1918. Mentioned in Dispatches, August 1918. *(London Gazette,* September 8th, 1918.) Next of kin, Sister. Eileen Joyce Harman, 14 Countess Road, Upminster, Essex."

"It's a good record for a youngster," said Petrella. "They put them into the thick of it pretty young in those days, didn't they?"

"I should think that by the spring of 1918 the army were glad to take anyone with two arms and two legs. The point is, is it Ricketts?"

"It easily could be," said Petrella slowly. "It fits in most of the essential points. Ricketts was in his late fifties, and was known to have a good First War record. The only thing is, that I'm pretty certain Lundgren said he had the MM. Wouldn't that be in his papers? I mean, wouldn't it be in Bancroft's papers if Bancroft later changed his name to Ricketts?"

"It ought to be. But if Ricketts was a crook, he could easily have put up a medal ribbon he wasn't entitled to. But we're getting somewhere, now. If this next-of-kin 'sister' was already married, she must have been a few years older than Robert. So a search among the Bancrofts at Somerset House for a few years back may turn her up. Then perhaps we can get her marriage certificate. If she was married in church we can get the names of the witnesses and parents-in-law and so on. Plenty of possibilities there."

Petrella said, "Suppose we do find Bancroft and he isn't Ricketts?"

"I refuse to think about it," said Haxtell. "You get on down to Lincoln's Inn and remember that all lawyers are the natural enemies of the police."

"Well now, Sergeant Petrella," said Mr Harrowing. "I asked you to come down and have a chat, because I understand that you were not entirely satisfied with the police case."

Mr Harrowing had served for several years, during the war, in the Royal Navy, and was aware of the value of the attack direct.

Petrella blinked a couple of times, and said, "Oh, I think that's an exaggeration. Who told you that?"

"These things get about," said Mr Harrowing, pushing a large box of cigarettes in Petrella's direction. He did not feel able to explain that the information had first reached him through the indiscretion, at the lunch table, of a Metropolitan Police solicitor, so he said, "We couldn't help noticing that they didn't trust you in the box at the Old Bailey."

This was accompanied by a smile which robbed the remark of offence.

"There's nothing in that," said Petrella. "All that I could say about the body could be much better said by Dr Summerson."

"Quite so. You can no doubt tell me one thing, without being indiscreet. Is the police investigation still going on?"

"Yes. It's still going on."

Mr Harrowing leaned back in his chair. He had a long, brown, serious face with a good mouth and jaw at the bottom of it. The thinning hair was the only sign of his long desk life.

"I'm going to be quite frank with you," said Mr Harrowing, who apparently liked what he saw of Petrella, too. "In fact, I'm going to start by throwing away my best card. I have no intention of calling you to give evidence under subpoena. Indeed, how can I? I have no idea what you could be likely to say, and until I know that, I have no idea whether you wouldn't do my client's case more harm than good."

"I see," said Petrella. "It hadn't occurred to me – I'm no lawyer, of course – but I didn't imagine that any further question of giving evidence arose."

"In the ordinary way, it wouldn't. In nineteen cases out of twenty, the Court of Criminal Appeal considers the record and listens to what counsel has got to say."

"And doubles the sentence."

"Well, that's the popular idea. However, it has full power to listen to fresh evidence. It doesn't happen often, I agree. A great number of cases go before it merely on points of law. That the judge misdirected the jury, or something like that. And in murder cases the prisoner may anyway feel that the sentence he has received cannot easily be doubled."

"There's something in that," said Petrella.

"But there are rare cases in which the court will listen to fresh evidence. Evidence which has come to light since the trial." Mr Harrowing leaned back in his chair. "I think this might be one of them."

Petrella said nothing.

Mr Harrowing said, "I wonder if the man in the street realizes quite how difficult it really is to defend a person who is charged with murder. I don't mean that the police are unfair. It's just that they have a monopoly. There's only the one investigating machine, and they're running it."

Petrella felt himself going red. He said, "They are bound to answer any questions the defence asks them."

"Quite so," said Mr Harrowing gently. "But how are they to know *what* questions to ask?" He paused, and added, "In books it is of course quite simple. I believe that private detectives of great ability abound. Very often, having been invited down for the weekend, before the murder occurs, they are handily on the spot before the police arrive. They have friends in every walk of life, private laboratories at their disposal, and unlimited money. I can only say that I have never had the good fortune to meet one. The private detectives that I have been called upon to deal with have been different." Mr Harrowing paused again, and added, "Quite different."

Petrella said uncomfortably, "I do know exactly what you mean. You'll understand that I'm not a very senior member of the police force, and I couldn't give you any information or help without permission."

"Of course. I understand that."

"I can tell you – I have told you already – that investigations are still going on. They haven't reached any sort of conclusion, and strictly speaking they are not investigations of your case at all. But obviously, if anything does come of them, it's going to be to your advantage."

Mr Harrowing nodded.

"And it's just occurred to me that there's a way you can help. I shall probably get into trouble for even suggesting it, but I'm in such hot water already that a pint or two more's not going to make much difference. Could you arrange for an advertisement – it's the sort of thing solicitors always seem to be doing, so it wouldn't necessarily arouse any suspicion – one of those things that says that if Mr A will get in touch with a certain firm of solicitors he will hear something to his advantage?"

"*Times* and *Telegraph*," said Mr Harrowing, making a note. "I can do that. Who's your Mr A?"

"He's a Robert Lowry Bancroft." Petrella spelled it out and Mr Harrowing wrote it down carefully. "He was last heard of in 1918 when he was serving in the 9th Royal South London Regiment, in which he attained the rank of lance corporal and was mentioned in dispatches. "

"I suppose you can't tell me what it's all about."

"Not at the moment. But if you should happen to find him, I can assure you of this. It will be the best day's work you've done for your client yet."

When Petrella got back to Crown Road he found an official letter waiting for him. It was impressed with the stamp of the Commissioner's Office, and it said that Detective Sergeant

Petrella was to call at New Scotland Yard on the Monday following, at half past four in the afternoon, in case he wished to exercise the right open to him under Regulation 16 of Police Regulations of making an explanation personally to the chief officer of police of the matters alleged in the Misconduct Form of which particulars had already been supplied to him. The letter went on to say that Petrella would be well advised to consult his superior officer, who would inform him of his rights in the matter.

Petrella took this straight in to Haxtell, who said, "Damn. I thought there was a chance that we had succeeded in killing this. Evidently I was wrong. What are you going to do about it?"

"I'm certainly not going to put anything in writing," said Petrella. "What's likely to happen?"

"It's a sort of preliminary skirmish. They want to hear what you've got to say – "

"So that if they don't like it, they can give me the whole works later."

"That's right. My own feeling is that if you apologized to Kellaway and promised not to try to fight the war on your own in future, they'd let you off with a caution."

"Nothing doing," said Petrella. "In fact, I may have added another large blot to my copybook this morning."

He told Haxtell about the suggestion he had made to Mr Harrowing. If he thought this was going to provoke an explosion he was wrong.

"It's not a bad idea," said Haxtell. "In fact, it's a good one. There's something about an advertisement from a firm of solicitors, saying that if you get in touch with them you'll hear something to your advantage. All the same, if Bancroft's Ricketts, and if Ricketts is the sort of man I'm beginning to picture him as, I don't see him coming forward to stick his head into a noose."

"*He* won't. But what about his relations, or old army friends? A lot of them must still be living. People do see you from time

155

to time, however carefully you try to avoid them. What's to stop one of them coming forward?"

"I said it was a good idea," said Haxtell, "and I meant it. But I think you should have told me what you meant to do, and let us fix it through one of our own contacts."

"If I'd stopped to think about it," said Petrella, "I expect I would have, but it doesn't make a great deal of difference. Not to me personally, I mean. As soon as this case is finished I'm getting out."

Haxtell looked for ten whole seconds at the furious young man opposite him, and said, at last, "I think I should wait and see, first, what they do want to say to you down at headquarters."

"You know exactly what they'll say. Some stuffy old chief superintendent, who's lived with one finger in the Rule Book ever since he worked his way up off a beat, is going to point out that I have infringed sixteen different rules and regulations by daring to think for myself, and – "

"All right," said Haxtell placidly. "Don't take it out on me. And don't let's chuck the hand in before it's finished. I'm as keen as you are to know what really happened up at the reservoir. Let's find out that first and worry about your future afterwards."

When Petrella had taken himself off, Haxtell got up, kicked the waste-paper basket with beautiful accuracy up on to the mantelpiece, and said, "Damnation take the silly young idiot."

That evening, at six o'clock, Petrella was ringing the bell of Flat 5, 74 Parsons Road. The door was opened, and he was not surprised to see the white-faced girl. Under the lights of the tiny hall she looked younger and ghastlier than she had done in the street.

"Jean's inside," she said. "I'd better leave you alone now."

"I hope I'm not driving you out."

"It's not really big enough for three," said the girl.

She opened the door. It was the tiniest flat he had ever seen. Really, it was one small room, most of which was taken up by a bed, and the rest by two chairs, arranged in front of an electric fire. A cupboard, opening out of one of the side walls, was the kitchen. And at the far end an alcove, curtained with sea-green waterproof material, suggested a bathroom. The furniture, carpet and curtains looked as if they had been bought as a job lot in the Tottenham Court Road by someone with a robust taste in colours.

"I'm off," said the girl. "I've got to be back here at seven."

"This won't take long," said Jean. She was sitting in one of the armchairs, and had hardly looked round when Petrella came in. She sounded as if she had started the day tired, and had then got a lot tireder, and now was so tired that it had ceased to matter.

"Sit down," she said. "I'm sorry about all this secrecy. But you'll understand when I tell you, I daren't be seen talking to you."

"I'm sorry my reputation's as bad as that," said Petrella.

She took no notice of it. She was past the point where conversational gambits were picked up and tossed back again. There was something she had to say and she would say it, and that was all.

"You remember when you came to see me before the trial and asked me a question about Rosa. Whether she'd met Ricketts?"

Petrella said he remembered.

"Well, it was a pretty good guess. She'd been going with him for months. He was her boyfriend."

"He was *what?*"

"What I said. Sydney Ricketts. He was all her idea of what a man should be. Grey hair, good manners, plenty of money. Of course, he was a phoney. Most of the money was hers anyway. But she couldn't see that, not at first. I'm not sure you can blame her. She'd only got people like her husband and Boot to compare him with. He must have seemed quite something after that pair."

"Are you telling me that they were sleeping together?"

"That's right. When she went out nights, that's where she went. And another thing, he was looking after her 'stocking' for her. All the stuff she was meant to be keeping an eye on for Monk."

"Of course," said Petrella. "Of course. Under the floorboard in the kitchen. Don't mind me. Please go on."

"That's all there is, really. When I heard she'd been shot, I thought he might have done it. She'd been getting the idea that he'd been fiddling her over the jewellery. Selling it on his own account. If Monk got out, there'd have to be a showdown, wouldn't there?"

"Yes," said Petrella. Curtain after curtain was being ripped down, layer after layer of obscurity dispersed. The puppet figures growing harder and clearer. "Yes, of course there would. Why on earth didn't you tell me this before?"

"Why?" she said. "Because I was scared, of course. What do you think?"

"Scared of whom?"

"Of Howton, first of all. He'd been smelling round my place ever since you found the body. Then – "

"Yes," said Petrella. "But after we'd charged him you couldn't have done him anything but good by speaking."

"I didn't owe him anything. Besides – "

"Go on."

"I didn't want to talk against Ricketts. I believe Rosa was more scared of him than she was of Boot. And she was a girl who didn't scare easily."

Petrella said nothing. She could feel the anger and contempt in him, and she said, "Why should I take any chances? I didn't want anything more to do with either of them. I was sorry for Rosa, but she wasn't part of my life. You don't understand. How can you?" Her voice went up. "What it is, to be a woman, without much money, in London, on her own. Particularly when you get mixed up with those sort of people."

Petrella said, "You'd get protection."

"I would if I was rich, or important."

"That's not true," said Petrella furiously.

"All right," she said, "don't blow your top. I'm not saying anything about 'one law for the rich, and another for the poor'. That's daft. The law's the same for everyone. It's just that there isn't enough of it to go round. I've seen protection for people like me. It means the bobby on the beat being told to keep an eye out for trouble. That's all they can do. There isn't even a lock on our street door. Did you know that? And Boot had a key to my flat. Rosa gave him one. And if I'd asked the landlord to change the lock, I'd have had to tell him why. And I'd have been out of the flat at the end of the month. You don't understand. People like Boot and Ritchie don't have to use a razor on a girl. They make a little row where she lives and she's out in the street, or come along and kick up a fuss at work, and she's out of a job. What's the use of police protection then?"

"If that's right," said Petrella, as if he hated it, but had to say it, "I understand why you wouldn't want a character like me calling round too much at your flat, but there's still one thing I can't understand. Why are you willing to tell me this now?"

"But of course," she said. "None of it matters now. Boot's booked, isn't he? And Ricketts is dead."

In the sudden silence she looked up sharply.

"Isn't he?" she said.

15

Petrella's Version

Petrella woke at four o'clock that morning. London is never entirely silent. In the far distance an all-night lorry grumbled as it changed gear on the hill, heading for the Barnet bypass and the Great North Road. Nearer at hand a shunting engine fussed as it pulled a line of freight cars out of a siding at Helenwood Junction. Footsteps rang on the pavement. One of London's millions was going to or from his work under the pale street lamps.

Petrella turned over for the hundredth time. His head was full and felt hot, and he fancied he was running a temperature. He was trying to recapture a memory. It was not so much a dream as a picture, something visualized on the fringes of waking and sleeping.

He was looking down from above on to the bank of the reservoir. It was late afternoon, but still very warm. They had had a true St Martin's summer that year. The gnats were singing a descant to the bumbling of the bees. In among the long, sun-dried grass, high up on the slope, a woman was lying. She was lying on her back, staring up at the unclouded sky. A butterfly drifted past and settled on her outstretched hand. He wanted to see whether she would move. Her hand stirred. The butterfly flew off. The woman rolled over onto her side.

There was a movement down on the path. Someone was coming. She raised herself on one elbow, to listen. Petrella forgot about the woman and concentrated his gaze on the point in the bushes at which the newcomer must appear. He had an urgent desire to see who it was. So had the woman. She craned forward so far that she obscured his view.

"Damn her," he said angrily. "She ought to take her hat off in the cinema." Then someone was shaking his arm, and it was broad daylight.

"You don't often oversleep," said Mrs Catt, his landlady. "I thought I hadden heard you on the move yet. You'll hardly have time for breakfus as it is."

Luckily Haxtell was late that morning too, so Petrella's defection escaped notice. The superintendent had had a telephone message and had gone straight from his house to the office of the director of public prosecutions, where he had spent half an hour with the director himself and had learned, without surprise, that the medical report on the killer of Corinne Hart had made it clear that he was unfit to plead.

As he was leaving, the director said, "I hear that Howton's solicitors have been nobbling one of your young men."

"That's right," said Haxteil cautiously. "He asked me about it, and I said he could go."

"I've no objection to his going," said the director, beetling his formidable eyebrows, "as long as he tells *us* anything he tells *them.*"

"I'm sure he'd do that," said Haxtell.

"I hope so. I gather that he is acquiring a reputation for being an independent-minded animal."

"He's an extremely hard-working and loyal officer," said Haxtell.

The director said "Hmmph," which Haxtell felt to be unfair as it might have meant anything at all.

Back at Crown Road Petrella was waiting for him, and he quickly learned what had happened the night before.

"Do you think she was telling the truth?" he said.

"Why, yes," said Petrella. In fact, he had not even thought about it. "Why should she lie?"

"She might have been put up to it by Howton's friends. As a last desperate move to get him off. Sow a bit of doubt."

"I don't think they would have had the wit to think it up and I don't think she would have done it if they had."

"All right," said Haxtell. "You're more likely to know if she's telling the truth than I am. You've seen her. I haven't. Let's start from there. Ricketts was Mrs Ritchie's lover, and she was carrying his child."

"He was more than a lover," said Petrella. "He was a safe deposit as well. He was hiding the jewellery for her which her husband had stolen and had entrusted to her before he went to prison. He had made a cache for it in the kitchen."

He told Haxtell about that.

"And you spotted this when you were on one of your – er – night-diving operations."

"I ran my finger into the butt end of the screw," said Petrella. "There's the scar. I didn't connect it with anything in particular at the time. It might have been something to do with the gas or electricity. And anyway it was empty."

"All right," said Haxtell. "Let's try to sort it out a bit. Start on Saturday afternoon. Take it slowly."

"I think," said Petrella, "that Rosa didn't go straight from her flat to the reservoir. According to Mrs Fraser, she was out of the house by three o'clock, but I don't think she got to the reservoir much before dusk."

"Because she'd have been seen climbing in."

"Yes, and because it was their routine. She'd go in much the same way that we did, across the far corner of the recreation ground, through the broken gate, and to a pre-arranged rendez-vous among the bushes."

"You think they'd met there before."

"Oh, I think so, yes. That was where he made love to her. One of the places." Petrella announced this with such curious conviction that Haxtell looked at him, but only said, "Well, we know she didn't go absolutely straight to the reservoir."

"How's that, sir?"

"She must have stopped somewhere to buy an evening paper. That edition she was carrying is on the streets, in the West End, at three o'clock, but it doesn't get up to these parts much before four."

"Right. And she'd taken out the middle sheet, with the piece about her husband on it, ready to show to Ricketts. And folded the rest of the paper away, out of sight. I think she was in a very dangerous frame of mind. Frightened, and angry. Angry with Ricketts, because he'd got her into trouble. Now that her husband was loose, it really was trouble. And angry because she'd begun to suspect that he'd been short-changing her about the jewellery."

"Selling it for his own account?"

"Yes. That was one thing I noticed about the jewellery sales. The only ones which are definitely tied up with Howton took place *after* the murder."

"And were quite small pieces. The idea being that he – all right, don't let's jump the gun. Go on. She's lying among the bushes, in a bad frame of mind, waiting for Ricketts to appear."

"Which he does. I think she stopped for something else too. I think – but this is pure guessing – that she met her husband. They arranged it when they spoke on the telephone the night before. I should think he wanted to see her a lot more than she wanted to see him, but she couldn't very well say no."

"You mean, she was afraid he might have heard about her and Ricketts? About the baby?"

"I don't honestly think that he would have cared very much if he had. It wouldn't have made him any fonder of Ricketts, I agree, but there was only one thing on his mind at the moment, and that was ready money. The money that she was supposed to have from the sale of the jewellery he had left with her, and which, as she had begun to realize lately, she was seeing very little of. Because Ricketts was doing the actual selling, and Ricketts was hanging on to most of the money."

Haxtell took time out to consider this. Then he said, "Do you suppose she told her husband about that?"

"I don't think she had any option. The one thing she couldn't explain away was that she ought to have had a lot of ready money – which he desperately needed at that moment – and she couldn't produce it."

"It's conjecture," said Haxtell. "But I think it's reasonable. So what did they plan to do?"

"What would you have done, sir?"

"Gone and shaken Ricketts down."

"And that was what they were going to do, too. She would go to her usual rendezvous with him, at dusk. That would give Monk a chance to get into the cottage. For that's where the remains of the jewellery and the ready money were. No doubt about that. If Ricketts had a hoard, it was in the cottage. Once he had been drawn away from the cottage, Monk was on to a good thing to nothing. Either he found what he was looking for. Or, if he didn't, he waited till Ricketts came back. There'd have been ways of making him talk."

"Yes. And what went wrong?"

"What must have gone wrong," said Petrella, *"is that Ricketts bought himself an evening paper too."*

There was a long silence, while Haxtell turned it all over in his mind. At the end of it, he let his breath out slowly, like a man who has come up from deep water, and said, "It's an idea. That would be why he took a loaded gun with him to his rendezvous. A war souvenir, that he kept, all greased up and loaded, and tucked away under another floorboard. Do you know, I'm beginning to get the impression that Mr Ricketts isn't a very nice character."

"His first wife was afraid of him," said Petrella. "And he impressed himself so powerfully on Jean Fraser, who, as far as we know, never even met him, that she wasn't prepared to say a word against him until she thought he was dead."

"I like this story," said Haxtell. "Go on, Patrick."

"I don't know whether Rosa lost her temper with him or whether he deliberately provoked her, but there certainly came a moment in their talk when she pulled out the folded page of the paper, and pushed it in his face, and said, 'You're not dealing with a helpless woman now. My husband's out, and he's in the cottage waiting for you, so you'd better come clean, or else –'"

"So he shot her."

"Yes. Quietly, there and then, all among the grass and the flowers, and shovelled a lot of leaves on her, and let her lie."

"And then went back to the cottage and dealt with Monk too."

"I think so. It was either that or give up the money. He'd killed once. He'd nothing to lose by killing again. I should think he had everything pretty well packed up for a getaway. An escape route mapped out. A hideout arranged."

"Yes. And it's clear why he dumped the second body in the reservoir. It would be a lot less messy and leave fewer traces than dragging it up into the bushes. And if he was going to dump the body, it was sensible to dump the gun as well. What I can't see is why, having dumped them, he didn't come back, tie up the boat, and walk quietly out of the front – oh, yes I can, though. The rest of the boys had turned up."

"That *must* be the answer, sir. There he is, sitting quietly, resting on his oars, in the middle of the reservoir, when – he hears something – sees a light in the cottage, perhaps. He can't go back, so he goes on. He'd know all about that back way out. He'd probably reconnoitred it earlier, with the idea of making a quick getaway. "

"And Howton? How much did he know or guess about all this?"

"He certainly didn't know about Rosa and Ricketts. He's got a tongue in his head, and if he'd known about it, it would have been one of the first things he'd have told his lawyer. My guess would be that Monk had simply told Howton he was going to the reservoir to meet his wife."

"Or he was seen – or followed. And Howton arrived too late, but in nice time to carry the can for everything. He'd ransack the cottage, no doubt. And he found what was left of the jewellery – the odds and bits that hadn't been worth selling before. And being a greedy bastard, he couldn't resist selling them himself. Thus wedging his ugly head firmly into a noose."

They walked around the structure for a bit, prodding it and picking at it.

"It's a nice build-up," said Haxtell. "Very creditable. How did you think of it all?"

Petrella nearly said that he'd seen the essential parts of it in a dream, but he realized in time that this would only increase his growing reputation for eccentricity.

"It came to me in bits and pieces," he said.

"I'm not sure I don't like it better than the official version, really," said Haxtell.

"Of course you do," said Petrella indignantly. "This is the truth."

"They're both theories. There's just one thing will clinch yours and destroy the opposition. Find Ricketts and fingerprint him. If it's his print on the gun – there's no argument."

"That's not going to be all that easy," said Petrella. "Even if Central showed more signs of co-operating, which they aren't."

Haxtell felt unable to pursue that one. But he knew, quite well, that a nationwide search with the drive of Scotland Yard behind it was a great deal more likely to be successful than any efforts they could organize themselves.

He said, "The more I think about Ricketts the more certain I am that he's that rare sort of criminal, a man who looks ahead. I believe we shall find that he had his hideaway all ready. It'd be a lot easier for him if he had someone to help him. An old mother, or a sister, or a fourth wife, or something of that sort. He'd visit her from time to time, and he'd be known, under some other name of course, as her son or brother or what have you. Then all he'd have to do would be to walk away from the reservoir, put on a pair of horn-rimmed glasses or a deaf aid or a toupee, or make some other slight adjustment in his appearance – just enough to cover himself if we decide to publish a photograph – and sink comfortably into his new background. That's the clever way to run away. Sit still."

The two men stared out of the window. It had begun to rain in the cold, vertical manner peculiar to England at this time of the year.

"He's careful, all right," said Petrella. "Almost brilliantly so. That telegram he sent was a real beauty. It worked both ways. If no suspicions were aroused, then it was just Ricketts saying goodbye to his employers. If people ever did get suspicious, then it could be something very different. The man who had disposed of Ricketts, covering up his tracks."

"That theory wasn't going to survive the dragging of the reservoir."

"Why not?" said Petrella, "Nothing might have come to light for a year or more. Perhaps until the Water Board made their next two-yearly tidying up of the shrubbery. I know that our fingerprint people are good – but, good heavens, after a year underwater who was going to say that the drowned man wasn't Ricketts?"

"It's no good sitting here telling each other what a damned clever chap he is," said Haxtell. "What we've got to do is to get busy and find him. And we've got – what's today? – Saturday."

"And the appeal's on Thursday."

"Then we've got five days to do it in. You can do a lot in five days if you give your mind to it."

"One thing," said Petrella, "that I am prepared to bet my bottom dollar on. If we're right about the sort of man Ricketts is, the very last thing he's likely to do is answer our advertisement."

The telephone rang. Haxtell picked it up, listened for a moment, and said, "What? Yes, he's with me. He can take the call from here." And to Petrella, "It's your lawyer pal."

Petrella picked up the telephone, and Haxtell unashamedly picked up the extension receiver.

"Harrowing here," said the voice thinly. "I thought I'd ring you, in case you missed it. We managed to get that advertisement in both papers this morning. Did you see it? They can't usually do it without twenty-four hours' notice. But I told them it was urgent."

"That's good work," said Petrella. "I hadn't seen them. *The Times* and *The Telegraph.*"

"That's right."

"And you'll get in touch with us if you hear anything."

Mr Harrowing sounded faintly surprised. "That's why I'm ringing you," he said. "I *have* heard something. A Mr Bancroft telephoned me just now. He's fairly certain from the details in the advertisement that he must be the man it refers to. He certainly managed to convince me. He wanted to know what it was all about. That put me in a bit of a difficulty."

"You say he telephoned you. Did he – did he give an address?"

"Oh, yes. An address in Hammersmith. I checked it. It's in the telephone directory. We might have thought of that, perhaps."

Petrella scribbled down the address and telephone number and said to Mr Harrowing, "Don't you worry. You've done very well. We'll look after this now."

"Can I – ?"

"If anything useful comes of it – useful to your client, I mean, you shall have it at once."

When the solicitor had rung off, they sat for a moment staring at each other.

"Let it be a warning to you," said Haxtell at last, "never to bet on certainties."

16

Infantry Soldier and Extra Wife

Riverside Fields, Hammersmith, which looks out across a strip of muddy foreshore at the ever-moving Thames, is a Hogarthian tumble of houses, some of them very big, some quite tiny, and all of them somehow lopsided and disreputable and flung down in a manner which would enchant a painter but distract the tidy heart of a town planner.

No. 50 was one of the tiny ones, no more than a four-room cottage. It was beautifully kept, its brass gleaming, its paint-work fresh, and Petrella felt no doubt at all that the woman who opened the door to him was Mrs Bancroft herself.

Equally, he felt little doubt that the small, wiry person who greeted him from a chair by the fire was Mr Bancroft. There was not an ounce of deception about either of them. No place in their lives, you would have said, was hidden from the light of day.

"It's about the advertisement," he explained.

"Quick work," said Mr Bancroft approvingly. "I only phoned after breakfast. What price the law's delays?"

"They can move when they have to," said Petrella. He added, "I'd better introduce myself. I'm a detective sergeant. I'll show you my papers, if you want to see them."

"Don't bother," said Mr Bancroft. The forenoon light was full on his face. He had shown no symptoms of alarm, only a vague interest. "I'd have come up to Lincoln's Inn myself, but my legs aren't so good, not when the weather's cold."

"Where do the police come into this?" said Mrs Bancroft.

"I'm not sure that we do," said Petrella. "Do you mind if I ask you a few questions?"

Mrs Bancroft looked as if she might mind, but her husband said, "Ask anything you like. Why not? It's a free country. You get us a cup of tea, Minnie."

Mrs Bancroft recognized that she was being dismissed and went reluctantly.

"Women talk too much," said Mr Bancroft. "Not but that she'll have it all out of me as soon as you've gone. Now then, what's it all about?"

"First of all," said Petrella. "Are you – or were you – Lance Corporal Robert Lowry Bancroft of the 9th Royal South London Regiment, who fought in France during most of 1918 and was mentioned in dispatches?"

"That's me," said Bancroft.

Petrella took carefully from his pocket a postcard-sized photograph of Howton. He handled it carefully, because the back of the photograph had been specially treated with a substance which, whilst impossible to detect by feel, was particularly receptive of fingerprints. He held it out to Bancroft, who grasped it trustingly.

"What am I supposed to do?" said Bancroft. "Say 'snap'?"

"I was wondering if you happened to recognize the man."

"Can't say I do. Ugly looking customer, ent he? Reminds me a little of the regimental sergeant major in the old South Londons. But o' course *he*'d be dead a long time now." Here he transferred the photograph thoughtfully to his other hand, to get a better light on it.

"Well, it was just a chance," said Petrella. He took the photograph gently back, put it into an envelope and dropped the envelope into his pocket. "Here's another question for you. I don't want to rake up the past more than I must, but did you get into a spot of trouble during your war service? Assault, or something of that sort."

"Trouble?" said Mr Bancroft. "CMPs – that sort of thing?"

"It might have started with the Military Police, but it ended up with a charge in a police court. It sounds like the sort of thing that might easily have happened while you were home on leave."

Mr Bancroft shook his head.

"It's a long time ago, I know," said Petrella.

"I wouldn't forget a thing like that," said Mr Bancroft. "All us boys had trouble with the Military Police, from time to time. But nothing that wasn't settled in the orderly room the next morning – and forgotten about a week later. I didn't have no trouble with the police. You look at my record, sometime. Honorable discharge. Character exemplary."

"I'm sure you're right," said Petrella, getting up. "There's been a muddle somewhere. And I'm only sorry you should have been troubled."

"No trouble. That bit about 'something to my advantage'. That was just put in to get an answer."

"Yes, it was, really. I'm terribly sorry – "

Mr Bancroft burst out laughing.

"I'm not the sort that has long-lost uncles turn up from Australia," he said. "I only had one uncle, come to that, and he was a lighterman and fell into the Thames at Chiswick and got drowned. I suppose you couldn't tell me what it's all about?"

Petrella felt tempted. Mr Bancroft, who might well have turned nasty, had been so unexpectedly nice that he felt that some sort of reward was due. Discretion prevailed.

"I can tell you this," he said. "It's a nasty case of murder. Double murder. We thought you might be able to help us – I'm quite clear now that it was a mistake – but if you had been the person we thought you were, it might have been very useful. And I'll come down here myself and tell you all about it as soon as we've got hold of the man who did it."

Mr Bancroft said unexpectedly, "You mean, that if I'd been able to tell you – something about that thing you were talking about – the case of assault – it might have been useful?"

"Very useful," said Petrella.

"Then why don't you?" said Mrs Bancroft, from the kitchen doorway.

They both stared at her.

"It's forty years buried, now. It can't harm you. If it can help, why not tell it?"

Outside, a child screamed shrilly. Mr Bancroft looked at his wife, opened his mouth, and shut it again.

"It's not a very creditable story," he said, and silence fell again.

Petrella sat down again, very gently, so as not to disturb Mr Bancroft's thoughts.

"It was in 1918. I had my birthday in January. I was just eighteen. I was due for the call-up sometime that spring, but I didn't wait for it. I went along. The first place I went to was an Intake Centre, at the old Crystal Palace. Then we moved down to Sussex. It was fun at first, waiting to go across. Then it wasn't so much fun. It was the wounded that unsettled us. The men who had been wounded before, going back again. One of those blew his foot off, in camp, the night before he was due for draft. That sort of thing isn't good for a young boy. It makes him edgy."

Outside, in the sunlight, the child screamed again. A long "Ya-ha-ha-ha". She was having fun, being a jet bomber.

"There was another young chap, enlisted the same day as I did. Name of Ricketts."

"Yes," said Petrella softly. "Yes. Go on, please."

"He was about the same age and height and shape as me. Same red cheeks and dark hair. I don't mean we were twins, but people who didn't know us sometimes mistook us. He was full of spirits. The whole thing was an adventure to him. Then a day or two before we moved to our embarkation camp, we had a final check – and they found he'd got something wrong with his ticker. No active service for Ricketts. No fighting, no fun. Clerical duties at the base. It broke him up. Can you guess the rest?"

"You did a swop."

"That's right. Names, clothes, kit, everything. Only one thing we kept. On the form we had to fill in before we sailed, we each put our own next of kin. Just in case anything happened."

"So he put down his – sister, wasn't it? And you put down your – ?"

"My aunt. What happened next was funny. Ricketts got sent straight out to the South Londons – a front-line crowd. That was in early March. I got my base job all right. Then we had the March push, when the Jerries nearly got to Amiens. By the time it was held, they were pretty hard up for men. So they had a recheck of all the medical categories."

"And found nothing wrong with you, and assumed the doctor at home had made a mistake."

"That's right, and buzzed me straight up to the front, to the old 9th. And the funny thing was," concluded Mr Bancroft, "that I believe I made a better soldier than Syd Ricketts after all. He got a 'mention' for me. *I* got an MM for him."

The story seemed to be at an end.

"What happened then?" said Petrella.

"Oh. When we were demobbed, we swopped back. We couldn't either of us say anything about it. We were both in the wrong, you see."

"The thing I don't like," said Mrs Bancroft judicially, "was him having your medal. It wasn't right. Particularly now it seems he left you a police record into the bargain. We didn't know about *that.*"

"But – " said Petrella. Then the absurdity of the whole situation struck him and he dissolved in laughter. Mr and Mrs Bancroft laughed with him.

"Do you mean," he said, "that no one ever knew? What about your families – I suppose you had to write a few letters?"

"Field Service postcards. And all you had to say was you'd hurt your hand and got a pal to write for you. There wasn't anything in any of them except 'I'm in the pink and I hope this finds you the same.' Anyway, my old aunt, who was the only relative I had, she died in April. Shock, they said, on account of a Zeppelin. She ought to have seen the old Blitz, eh?"

"Did Ricketts' sister ever write back to you?"

"Once or twice. A lot of home gossip and stuff, I can remember that. Only she was always pestering me for matchboxes."

"Matchboxes?"

"She collected 'em. Matchbox tops. I used to send her French ones, when I could get hold of them."

"And you've never seen Ricketts since."

"That's right. And I don't suppose I'd recognize him if I did. Nor him me. I used to be a bit nervous at first someone would turn the whole story up and I'd get into trouble. But the years went by and it got buried, and I don't suppose anyone would worry a lot about it now if they did know, would they?"

"I'm certain they wouldn't," said Petrella.

"Has it been any help to you?" said Mrs Bancroft.

"Well," said Petrella. "It's told us where not to look, and that's always a help."

"So all the time we were checking up on Rickett's army record it was really Bancroft?" said Haxtell.

"That's right, sir."

"And everything we found out about Bancroft belonged to Ricketts."

"Except the next of kin. They were genuine."

"And Bancroft – I mean Ricketts – no, I don't, I mean Bancroft got the MM that Ricketts wore in the Second World War."

"Yes. After all, it was a very safe fraud, from Ricketts' point of view."

"I think that makes it worse," said Haxtell. "What the hell are we going to do now?"

"Our best chance is the sister. If she's still alive."

"You think she might know where he is?"

"It's an odd sort of character who's emerging," said Petrella. He added apologetically, "I've been thinking about him a good deal, lately."

"Let's have it."

"This last little bit sort of sets the pattern, don't you think? He tried on this change of identities with Bancroft – and it worked. It didn't do him much good, but it came off. No one found out about it. Well, I think he's been doing things like that ever since. Living a piece of his life in one place, then cutting completely adrift and moving off somewhere else."

"Living on women?"

"Oh, yes. I should think so. And if that's right, he'd need a firm base to manoeuvre from."

"And that might be his sister."

"Yes. He would be her brother who 'lived abroad' and came home on long visits every now and then. It would be perfectly natural for him to turn up at any time, with a suitcase, and reoccupy the spare room that was always kept for him."

"And all we know about his sister is that she was called Mrs Harman in 1918. She may have changed her name six times since then. There's no law against it."

"We know she collected matchboxes," said Petrella.

That was Saturday evening.

On Sunday Petrella got a message from Sister Macillroth and went round to the hospital. At ten o'clock the night before Gover had sneezed twice and opened his eyes. He had passed as good a night as could be expected and was now fully conscious. Something in the sister's tone of voice made Petrella ask, "Will he be all right now?"

"That's impossible to say," said the sister. "That's what we want you for. Come along."

Gover was propped among pillows. His head, which had been shaved clean when he was operated on, had grown a stubble of hair during his long unconsciousness. There was a little more colour in his face, but not much. He looked like someone who has come back from the other side of the moon.

"Nice to see you awake, sir," said Petrella.

Gover looked at him for a long moment. Then his mouth cracked into a smile and he said, "Hullo, Patrick. How are things with you?"

"Fine," said Petrella, and found himself being ruthlessly hustled out again.

"Do you mean to say," he said indignantly, "that that's all you wanted me for?"

"We had to see if his memory was working. He wouldn't know any of us."

After this good start, the rest of the day dragged. That night Petrella hardly slept at all.

When he got to the station on Monday morning, Cobley said, "You've got a visitor. We put her in the interview room."

"What's it about?"

"No idea, Sergeant. It's a woman. She said it was to do with the Reservoir Case. The superintendent isn't here yet, so I told her you'd see her when you came in."

"Ricketts' sister?" said Petrella.

"Come again," said Cobley.

"Every time in this case," said Petrella, "that we've talked about someone and said, 'we shall never see *them,*' they've turned up almost at once."

A small woman rose from the chair in the interview room to greet him. Petrella thought she might be in her early thirties. She had a pretty face, spoiled only by a hardness of the mouth and the two vertical lines between the eyes which can be engraved by worry or pain. Her blue eyes were shrewd.

"Can we help you?" said Petrella.

"I don't know if I can help you, or you can help me," said the woman. "I'm Mrs Ricketts."

"Mrs Ricketts?"

"That's right. Sydney Ricketts' wife."

"When – ?"

"In 1946. In the Marylebone Registry Office."

It suddenly occurred to him that he didn't know what to say. She saved him the trouble.

"You're going to tell me he's married already," she said. "Is that right?"

"Yes," said Petrella. "If we're talking about the same man."

She fished in her handbag and pulled out a photograph. It was a snapshot, taken on the beach. It showed a man, lying back on the sand, on his elbows, laughing; a good figure of a man, despite advancing middle age; a nice, easy, indeterminate face.

"I've never seen Ricketts or a photograph of him," said Petrella. "But I can soon show this to someone who has."

"He was funny about photographs," said the woman. "He'd never have one taken. If there was anyone about him with a camera he'd keep out of their way. When he found out I'd taken this one, he got hold of the negative and the print and tore them up. I never told him I'd kept a spare print. As a matter of fact, that was what first made me wonder about him. That and the fact that he was so mysterious about his family."

"You never met any of them?"

"Met them? I never even heard him speak about them. I asked him once or twice, but I soon gave up. Wait a minute, though. When I say never, I'm wrong. Once – it was soon after our marriage – we passed a little girl in the street wearing one of those iron things round her leg and a great heavy foot. I said something – 'What a handicap it must be.' He said, 'My sister's been like that since she was a baby, and she's had a very happy life.' "

"You gathered she was still alive?"

Petrella's eagerness had betrayed him. She stopped, and looked at him.

"Suppose you tell me something first," she said. "You can guess why I'm here. I read that piece in the papers, about him being found drowned. Was it true?"

For a moment he hesitated. Then a look from her sharp eyes decided him.

"No," he said. "That was just the newspapers. The truth would have to come out as soon as they had the inquest. It wasn't Ricketts, it was – someone else."

"So he's done the disappearing trick again."

"Yes," said Petrella. "He's done it again." (How many times before, how many times since?) "When did he walk out on you?"

"In 1949. As soon as we'd spent all my money."

"I see."

"And he didn't walk out on me. I walked out on him."

He looked at her.

"You probably won't believe this bit," she said. "It was early in 1949. We had a flat, at Romford, and he was travelling for Barshalls, the sweet people. But it's no good asking them about him, because I tried that later, and they didn't know a damned thing. I was saying – it was one evening, when we were going to bed. We'd had a quarrel. We didn't quarrel a lot. He was an easy man to live with – but we'd had a quarrel that night, about my money. And it went on in the bedroom. I was sitting on a stool, in front of the dressing table, doing something to my hair. And I said – I can't remember the exact words – something about it was no good him thinking he could spend all my money and then walk out on me. He married me, and I was his wife, and that was something that lasted for life. And he said, quite quietly, 'Yes, of course.' It wasn't what he said, it was just that I happened to look in the glass at the moment, and caught the expression on his face. It was – it was quite cold. Like a reptile. I'd never seen a look like it before, on a human face, and I never want to again. The next day I packed up my things and walked out on him."

17

Central

"It doesn't tell us a great deal we didn't know already," said Haxtell. "It fills out the picture a bit."

"I'm beginning to visualize Ricketts," said Petrella.

"He fits into a sort of pattern, doesn't he? Living on women, spending their money, then cutting adrift."

"The second Mrs Ricketts cut adrift from him. He scared her stiff."

"He seems to specialize in scaring women. Now. What have we got – ?"

"We've got a photograph. I thought I'd check it with Lundgren at once, and then we could have it enlarged and duplicated."

Haxtell stared down at the snapshot on the desk. From the fading print, the man laughed back at him. Haxtell said, "He's a handsome old goat, isn't he? He's got what all women go for, Patrick. You know what that is? It's the relaxed look. It doesn't matter if you spend all her money, beat her, rob her baby's china money box – as long as you're relaxed about it, she'll love every moment of it."

"I bet he's relaxing right now," said Petrella. "And I've got an increasing hunch that he's with that sister of his, taking things easy, planning his next foray."

"If she's still alive."

"She was alive in 1946. And we know one more thing about her, now. She was born with one leg shorter than the other, and she has to wear a thick boot."

"Unless Ricketts was making that up, too."

"He's quite capable, blast him."

"I'm beginning to think – " said Haxtell, when the telephone interrupted him. It was not a long conversation. It consisted mostly of Haxtell saying "Yes", and at the end, "All right."

"You're wanted down at the Yard," he said. "As soon as possible. You can take a car."

"Are you sure that's right? I was due down there at four o'clock for a – whatever it is is going to happen about Kellaway's complaint."

"I don't know about that. All I know is that the assistant commissioner has expressed a desire to have a word with you."

Petrella gaped at him.

"I'm not pulling your leg. You'd better get a move on. He's a bad man to keep waiting."

"I understand," said Romer, his long, hatchet face expressionless, "that there have been developments in the Binford Reservoir Case since the hearing at the Central Criminal Court. I'm told that you have been the officer most actively engaged, and it seemed to me that the best way of bringing myself up to date was by having a word with you. If we're going to change our minds about Howton, we haven't a lot of time to do it in."

Petrella made what he hoped was going to be a non-committal noise. It sounded so terrible that he swallowed it, half uttered.

"What I'd like you to do is to tell me exactly what you think did take place. You needn't waste time over the background. I've read the file."

So Petrella told him. Once he had got started, it was not difficult. He had told it to himself so often that it came tripping out like a favourite story, almost too word-perfect for complete conviction. At the end of it Romer said, "So your view is that Howton was there that night, but that he turned up too late to do anything but collect some oddments of jewellery – and to put himself on the spot by selling them later."

"Yes, sir. The people who gave evidence of sales by Howton all spoke of the last two months. And the pieces involved were quite small. Mr Robins, for instance, only gave him a hundred pounds for six of them. Even at the usual rate of discount, that's not big stuff."

"Your idea is that Ricketts had already sold anything that was worthwhile. And that if we took the witnesses who had failed to identify Howton and confronted them with Ricketts they would identify him."

"I think so, yes, sir."

"And that the fingerprint found on the gun will turn out to be Ricketts'. Wrongly filed here, incidentally, as belonging to Bancroft."

"Yes, sir."

"And that the people who identified the gun as being Howton's weren't entirely reliable witnesses."

Petrella could easily have gone wrong there. But the last few months had taught him a lot of lessons. He said, "It was a very common type of gun, sir. It would be quite easy to be mistaken about a thing like that."

"Yes," said Romer. "It would. The Crown, on the other hand, maintains that Howton did arrive in time. That he shot both Ritchie and his wife, and disposed of the bodies. The facts which have now come to light about Ricketts living with Mrs Ritchie – and living on her – affords an explanation, which was missing before, of why he ran away when it came to the pinch. They don't necessarily make him a murderer."

"No, sir."

"In fact, there are two theories. And there's only one way of discovering which is right. We've got to find Ricketts." He unfolded his long body and took it across to the bow window which looked down on Westminster Pier and the pleasure boats.

"And you have a photograph, and you think he may be living with his sister, who has a deformity of the leg."

"And collected matchboxes," said Petrella. "According to Bancroft."

"Well, we've got home with less than that before now. We'll see what we can do. Thank you."

As Petrella turned to go, Romer added, "I nearly forgot. There's been a disciplinary complaint against you over your conduct in this case." He picked up a thin, Oxford-blue folder from his desk. "I have read the papers. I have an overriding discretion in all such matters. And I have decided that, although you acted in disobedience of orders, those orders were not, themselves, very sensible. I have given instructions for the record to be destroyed."

Petrella could think of nothing to say.

"Don't imagine, however, that I condone direct disobedience. It's a thing you can get away with only once in your professional career. Always supposing you intend to continue in your career. Superintendent Haxtell said something about your resigning."

"No, sir," said Petrella. "That was a mistake."

"I'm glad about that," said Romer.

On his way out Petrella ran into Sergeant Blinder, who said, "Oh, there you are. I understand you've been upsetting the Fingerprint System, now. If you've thought up something better, you might let me know."

"Hadn't you heard?" said Petrella. "It's all being changed."

"All – ?"

"The whole thing. Fingerprints are out. Everyone is to be classified by their electronic reflective index. The new American system. It's quite infallible – "

"Tcha!" said Sergeant Blinder.

Petrella went on his way. Outside Scotland Yard, between the western entrance and the Cenotaph, there stands a public house where generations of policemen have slaked their thirst. Petrella found Sergeant Dodds propping up the saloon bar.

"What cheer, Patrick," said Dodds. "Wattle it be?"

"Oh, half a pint," said Petrella cautiously.

"Pint of bitter for my friend," said Dodds. "I've got some news for you."

"You've decided to turn over a new leaf."

"I've turned over so many of those," said Dodds, "that I've pretty nearly finished the book. No – it's Chris. He's handed in his cards."

"Chris?"

"Who else? Said he couldn't afford to stay on a minute longer. His publishers are roaring to go, and he's getting a personality spot on TV. It's all fixed. Well, I ask you! Bungho."

"Bungho," said Petrella.

"His first book's out in the autumn. *Murder, Mayhem, and Mirth* it's called. I get two mentions in it. 'My old friend Albert Dodds agreed with me' – page ninety-two, and 'Sergeant Dodds expressed a contrary view' – page a hundred and four."

"I believe you're making the whole thing up."

"Cross my heart, I'm not. It'll be in the *Gazette* tomorrow." Sergeant Dodds picked up three darts from the counter and flung one of them idly into the dartboard. "One case I don't mind betting he leaves out though, that's the Binford Reservoir Case. Between you and me, it wasn't really one of our best."

The second dart followed the first, landing a fraction of an inch from it.

A sharp-looking character removed himself from the end of the bar, rolled forward, and said, "Either of you gentlemen interested in a game of darts?"

"Well, I'm not much of a hand at it," said Sergeant Dodds, throwing the third dart which, curiously enough, missed the board altogether. "But I don't mind having a game if you insist."

The sharp gentleman produced a well-worn set of darts from a leather container, and threw one into the centre of the board. It landed in the 25. Sergeant Dodds, without taking apparent aim, threw his dart into the 50, and said, "That gives me the start. I usually play for five bob a leg, ten bob on the game. OK?"

Petrella left hastily.

18

A Day Trip

To all Stations of the Metropolitan Police Force and to all Chief Constables of Borough and County Forces: Most Urgent. It is desired to trace a lady, at one time passing under the name of Eileen Joyce Harman. Thought to be between fifty-five and sixty-five years of age and to be suffering from a deformity of one leg necessitating the wearing of a surgical boot...

Tuesday was a difficult day. Even Haxtell had little idea of what was happening and, being a wise man, turned himself grimly to routine. The successive impact of Corinne Hart and the Reservoir Case had disrupted the divisional detective work at Highside and a half dozen of more or less routine jobs were piled up for his consideration.

Petrella found it impossible to cultivate the same detachment. The fact that nearly three dozen milk bottles were missing from Argos Road and the coin box of a telephone kiosk on Helenwood Common had been broken open and rifled failed to monopolize his attention. In the afternoon he gave up trying and made an excuse to slip over to Hounds Green.

Mr Lundgren was surprised, but evidently pleased, to see him.

"I've been meaning to get hold of you," he said. "My wife and I were wondering if you could join us in a game of bridge one evening."

Petrella said there was nothing he would like more, but did not deceive the kindly resident engineer.

"You didn't come over here to talk about bridge," he said. "What's on your mind?"

"It's Ricketts," said Petrella.

"You've found out where he is?"

"No," said Petrella. "I mean, yes. I can't tell you anything about this new development, not just at the moment. What I wanted to do was to have a look at the things Ricketts left behind. I remember you told me you'd got them."

"They're in the basement, here. You can look at them now if you'd like. There's not a lot. We'll pick the key up from the desk. It struck me at the time as rather odd – "

"What was that?"

"Well, I rather gathered, from what you told me and what I read in the papers, that the idea was that Ricketts was so upset by the goings-on that night that he left in a flurry. If that's right, isn't it remarkable he left so little behind? Wait there a moment, while I switch the light on?"

"Ricketts was a remarkable man," said Petrella. "I don't believe he did anything in a flurry. A hurry, perhaps, not a flurry. I imagine that his departure was most carefully planned. I don't mean that he knew exactly when he was going to leave, but he always visualized that he might have to pull out sometime, and quickly."

"That's exactly the impression you'd get from looking through his things. He didn't leave a stitch of clothing except the stuff which was actually at the laundry. You'll find everything he did leave in that big packing case. And there's really nothing that you could call a personal belonging. Just sheets and pillowcases, and two sets of curtains and some crockery and cooking stuff. Most of it bought from local shops. I imagine. In fact, I remember he had to have all his meals out, to start with. So he can't have brought much household stuff with him when he came. That rug was in the front of the fire in the sitting-room. Not in very good taste, is it? Another odd thing. The man who cleared up for us commented on it. He didn't find a single scrap of paper. Even the waste-paper basket had been emptied."

"It was too much to expect that he'd make any obvious mistakes. I did have a faint hope that as his actual departure was so quick he might have forgotten something – "

"We found these gardening things in the shed. He was a keen gardener. Did a lot of digging. And I seem to remember that he was a bit of a handyman, too. He had a plane and a good set of chisels. But those seem to have gone with him. What – ?"

He broke off. His audience was no longer with him. Petrella was on his knees in front of the now nearly empty packing case. Slowly he dipped into it, slowly drew forth a pink vase, ornamented with tiny green oyster shells; shells which formed the words *"A Present from Whitstable"*.

"By God," he said at last. "It's a chance."

By twelve o'clock the next morning the chance had grown into a bare possibility.

Superintendent Denmark, the chief officer of the Whitstable and Herne Bay Constabulary, had started with considerable scepticism about the whole project.

"Millions of souvenirs like that sold every year," he said. "All it means is that this man knew somebody who had once spent a holiday at Whitstable. Isn't that right?"

"It's only a chance, of course," said Petrella.

"Or he may have spent a holiday here himself. Of course, we'll do what we can. I saw the teletype. Wasn't much real information there, was there now?"

"It was all we had," said Petrella humbly. He was in no position to command. The successful working out of his hunch depended entirely on the co-operation of this fiery little man with the ginger-coloured moustache adhering like a blob of bitter marmalade to his aggressive upper lip.

"What did occur to me," said Petrella – "I expect you'd had very much the same idea – was that we might get at it through the doctor's. People who have a deformity like that have to have a regular check-up. It isn't the foot itself. It's the hip – "

"Yes. That wouldn't be too difficult. We could get a list from the doctor's."

It turned out to be quite a long list. Fortunately a number of candidates could be disposed of at once. Either they were the wrong age, or the wrong sex, or other disqualifying circumstances arose.

"Can't be Mrs Toomey," said Denmark. "She's related to my mother. A most respectable old lady."

Mrs Toomey was struck off the list.

By the afternoon there were three real possibilities left. All of them were ladies of past middle age, about whose background little was known. And all of them had at least one gentleman of approximately the same age recently come to stay with them, in the capacity of family, lodger, or paying guest.

"Well, there you are," said Denmark. "Short of calling on them, I don't know how you're going to pick the winner. What's he done, by the way? I ought to have asked you that before."

"The known charges," said Petrella, "are double murder and bigamy. There might be further charges of larceny to follow."

"I shouldn't worry about any further charges myself," said Denmark. "If you're going visiting, you'd better have one of my men with you."

"If we do find him, sir, we shall have to go gently. He's a very clever man, very alert, and ready to disappear at the drop of a hat. I think, if you don't mind, I'd like to make a little preliminary reconnaissance first. I promise I won't move without letting you know."

The next two hours were busy, and at the end of them he had dismissed Mrs Cartland from his calculations. He had seen the male relative who had recently joined her at Whitstable, and he had turned out to be a pale young man, very little older than Petrella himself. On the other hand, as between Mrs Williams and Mrs Duhamel, there was still very little to choose. Both were of the right age, both wore undeniable surgical boots, both took in occasional summer boarders and both had been joined "about two months ago" by a gentleman a little younger than themselves.

It was at the general stores, where he was pursuing his inquiries in the character of a prospective lodger, that a genuine inspiration visited him.

"I wonder," he said, "if that would be the Mrs Duhamel I knew in Yarmouth. It's not a common name, is it?"

The assistant agreed that it wasn't a common name. He imagined it might be French.

"One thing I do remember about her. If it's the same woman, that is. She had a fine collection of matchboxes. "

The assistant shook his head. He had never heard anything like that about Mrs Duhamel. As Petrella turned away disappointed, he added, "Of course, if it had been Mrs Williams now – "

"Does Mrs Williams collect?"

"*Does* Mrs Williams collect," said the assistant. "There's scarcely a day goes by but she's in here bothering us for a new sort. Of course, we're very sorry for her, with her infirmity, poor lady, but sometimes when we're rushed with customers – "

But Petrella was already out of the shop. At the eleventh hour, after all rational chances had failed, after all the favourites had tumbled, a real, genuine, hundred-to-one outsider had come romping home. He wished Bill Borden had been there. They could have had a drink on it.

"It certainly sounds hopeful," said Denmark. "Now let's do a bit of thinking. Bay View – that's the line of small houses actually on the front. Number 36 would be pretty nearly the end one. There's an open stretch of sand dunes at one side. We'll have to guard that. And a sort of pleasure park – it's shut just now – at the back. Two men there. And one man along the sea wall on the other side. We needn't worry about the front. He won't swim. Not in this weather."

Petrella was glad to see that the superintendent was taking the job seriously. He had a feeling about Ricketts which was beginning to border dangerously on the superstitious; that he was no ordinary man but a creature with curious instincts of his own, attuned to danger and sensitive to threats.

"Do you think he's carrying a gun?"

"I don't know, sir. He could be. He's used one before."

"I think we'll keep quiet about that. Don't want to make my people nervous. Now, then – as soon as we're all in position we'll walk up the front steps and knock at the door. You've got that photograph. Think you can identify him?"

"Oh, yes," said Petrella. "I'm sure about that."

He couldn't have said why he was so sure.

It was five o'clock by this time. The wind, which had been blowing great guns all day, had blown the clouds out of the sky, and a pale sun was now looking down on a wrinkled grey sea.

As Petrella and the superintendent approached No. 36 the front door, which stood at the head of a little flight of steps, opened gently, and Ricketts came out. He was wearing a soft cap, of old-fashioned cut, a muffler, twisted twice round his neck, with the ends tucked well down inside his coat, and he was carrying a stick. Petrella had not the slightest doubt who it was. He had made no sign to the superintendent, but the superintendent knew, too. The two men walked on past the house. Out of the tail of his eye Petrella saw Ricketts come down the front steps, and turn towards the town.

As soon as they were out of sight they turned too. Three of the men they had posted were visible. The superintendent waved them after him, and hoped they would understand.

Pausing every now and then to take deep breaths of sea air, and once to purchase a packet of cigarettes, Ricketts made his way eastward with the concentration of a man who is following a known routine.

"Further he gets from home the better," said the super-intendent. "We'll take him when he turns."

But Ricketts showed no intention of turning. He walked steadily forward, keeping the sea on his left. Ahead lay the old harbour. Beyond that, the wastes of Tankerton.

When he reached the harbour, Ricketts swung left, out on to the short stone pier, and stood for an instant at the far end of it, outlined against a sky now lemon yellow under the setting sun, then turned back.

The two men barred his way.

"Excuse me," said the superintendent, "but is your name Ricketts?"

The man had stopped, a yard from them. He made no attempt to answer. He was looking to right and left, weighing chances, calculating risks. They might have had the world to themselves.

"Look out!" yelled the superintendent, and threw himself forward, as Petrella ducked forward; and the next moment rose, shamefacedly, from his knees. For what the man had produced from his pocket was an ordinary cherrywood pipe, which he proceeded calmly to fill.

"What's the big idea?" he said. "Weaving about like that. Yes. My name's Ricketts. Who the devil are you?"

19

In the Court of Criminal Appeal

Petrella sat alone in the crypt bar of the Royal Courts of Justice. It was eleven o'clock in the morning and he was drinking a cup of milky coffee.

Somewhere above his head, in that rambling wedding cake of a building, in the court of the Lord Chief Justice of England, the Lord Chief himself, assisted by Mr Justice Penworthy and Mr Justice Meiklejohn, was considering the case *of The Queen against Howton.*

Up to a late hour on the previous night – and Petrella's head still ached at the recollection of that endless conference, of the atmosphere made fouler by the pipe smoked by the director of public prosecutions, of Barstow's red face getting redder and redder as the hours went past – up, in fact, to the early hours of that morning it had not been decided precisely what action to take.

"The only absolutely cast-iron piece of evidence we've got," said the director, "is the print on the gun. That corresponds, as nearly as a seven-week-old fingerprint can be expected to correspond with anything, with the index finger of Ricketts' right hand. It's not a strong identification, but we'd probably get it accepted, if the rest of the case stands up."

"The rest of the case," said Barstow, "is that Ricketts was the dead woman's lover, had been chiselling her, and shot her and her husband when it came to a showdown."

"Shot her," said the director, gently, "with a gun which the Crown has recently spent a strenuous two days proving in court to be the property of Howton."

An uncomfortable silence had ensued.

"If only Ricketts wasn't so damned cool," said Barstow. "He hasn't made a shadow of a mistake since we took him inside." He added, petulantly, "Most murderers give themselves away as soon as they start opening their mouths."

The argument had gone round in a circle, and Petrella had slept, and woken with a guilty start, and found himself unnoticed, and slept again.

In the end the director had said, "We could ask for an adjournment. I'm against that. This isn't a case which is going to look any better in a week's time. We've got all the facts we're likely to get. It's simply the view we take of them. I'll have a word with the attorney general and Younger in the morning, and we'll abide by what they say. You'd better all stand by in case you're wanted."

So Petrella stood by. And ordered another cup of coffee.

The Reservoir Case, in its early stages, had failed to grip the public imagination. The victim was a woman, but not a young nor a glamorous woman. And the prisoner was a professional criminal, and seemed to be quite plainly guilty.

Now, no one quite knew how, at the last minute of the eleventh hour, the word had got through to Fleet Street that the Reservoir Case was news; news on the largest possible scale.

There had been an independent investigation – no one quite knew by whom. New facts had come to life. The reputation of the police was involved. There had been a hasty rereading of the reports of the case at the Old Bailey and a new significance had been seen in Mr Wainwright's attacks on Superintendent Kellaway. Had they really been so wide of the mark? Might there be something – ?

"Get down and see Howton's solicitors," said the editor of the *Trumpet*. "We'll make an offer for Howton's story." He mentioned a figure which caused the hard-working and underpaid reporter whom he was addressing to open his eyes very wide indeed. "If the Court of Appeal upholds the verdict, we may have wasted our money, but I think it's a gamble worth taking."

"Have our best man cover the appeal," said the editor of the *Outline*. "*I* heard in the club on very good authority that there's going to be a first-class stink. Even if they don't allow the appeal, there'll be some good stuff."

"Howton," said the editor of the *Basket*. "Never heard of him, but I'm told he's important – how do you spell it, by the way?" No one seemed to know. "We don't want to get left behind. Read up all the reports of the earlier hearing – and get cracking."

It had all happened so quickly that, although everyone knew, on the best authority, that something sensational was going to happen, no one quite knew what the fuss was about. Not that this worried the people concerned. Fleet Street works very happily when it is in a hurry.

Nothing was possible in the morning papers beyond a few guarded preliminary references. But by half past nine there was a queue for the public gallery, and when the three judges took their seats on the stroke of ten o'clock the court was crowded.

The Lord Chief Justice of England, Lord Melford of Drome, a short but unforgettably impressive figure, faced Boot Howton across the well of the highest Court of Criminal Jurisdiction in the land.

"I understand, Mr Younger," said the Lord Chief, "that in view of certain evidence now in its possession, the Crown has decided not to proceed with the case against this man."

"That is so, my Lord," said Mr Younger.

"Very well then, Mr Younger. It only remains – "

"Might I say a word, my Lord?"

"Certainly, Mr Wainwright. I take it you are not going to press the Crown to reconsider its decision?"

"I should only like it to be made plain, my Lord – I under-stand this to be the case – that this decision has not been reached on any legal technicality but because the Crown is now quite convinced that my client had nothing to do with the crime with which he stood charged."

The Lord Chief looked at Mr Younger, who rose again, and said, "That is so, my Lord. I would add that proceedings are pending against another accused."

"In that case," said the Lord Chief, "it remains only for me to discharge you. Which I do."

The next moment the dock was empty, and unparalleled confusion had ensued. The team from the *Trumpet,* who had come to watch over their protégé – (Howton had become theirs for a large down payment at nine o'clock that morning) – had barely settled in their places and were separated from the door of the court by a dense crowd. They made the best of their way towards the nearest exit, but unfortunately there were a number of other people with the same idea in mind, to say nothing of the legal advisers in the next case on the list, who were caught equally unprepared and were moving strongly in the opposite direction.

"If there is any further disturbance," said the Lord Chief, "I will have the court doors locked, and anyone who is in will stay in, and anyone who is out will stay out."

Petrella had just put down his empty cup and was wondering how he was going to kill the hours until lunchtime when a small, lancet-shaped door with intricate iron hinges a few feet away from him opened, and Howton came out. He was quite alone, and looked a bit lost.

The two men stared at each other speechlessly.

A court official appeared behind Boot, and said to him, "If you want to avoid the crowd, you can slip out into Carey Street."

"That's all right," said Howton. He stood, still staring at Petrella, and Petrella stared, fascinated, back.

A faint sneer ridged Howton's unlovely face. "So you couldn't make it stick," he muttered. Then he hitched himself round, and stumped off, up the tiled passage, and through the swing doors at the end of it, and out of sight.

Petrella sat on for a long time. He was tucked away at the end of the long bar, and no one took any notice of him. He watched the team from the *Trumpet* go past, faint but pursuing; and a group of solicitors' managing clerks, with nothing much to do but drink Bass and Guinness, and various members of the public who seemed to have lost their way.

A fresh bustle of activity round the bar signalled that the luncheon recess was approaching. He got up stiffly and walked out into the main hall of the courts.

On an impulse he turned left halfway down the hall, climbed a flight of turret stairs straight out of grand opera, and found himself immediately outside the Lord Chief Justice's court.

He pushed open the door and peered inside. The court was empty, and silent, but it had the signs of its recent use all about it; the heavy chairs on the dais pushed back, just as their judicial occupants had quitted them; the clerk's table below the dais littered with papers; and books everywhere, some lying singly, some strapped in bundles, and many thousands more cramming the shelves which walled the court. Petrella thought that he had never seen a room more impressive or more apt to its purposes: panelled, cool, a quiet harmony of law-calf and boxwood set against green curtains and walls.

Immediately over the Lord Chief's seat, carved in hardwood, the Lion and the Unicorn faced each other across the Crown. The Unicorn was gazing up into the ceiling. The Lion, on the other hand, was staring down his nose at the court. He had a sardonic look about him. He had been watching over Justice for so long.

MICHAEL GILBERT

CLOSE QUARTERS

An Inspector Hazlerigg mystery

It has been more than a year since Canon Whyte fell 103 feet from the cathedral gallery, yet unease still casts a shadow over the peaceful lives of the Close's inhabitants. In an apparently separate incident, head verger Appledown is being persecuted: a spate of anonymous letters imply that he is inefficient and immoral. When Appledown is found dead, investigations suggest that someone directly connected to the cathedral is responsible, and it is up to Hazlerigg to get to the heart of the corruption.

'…brings crime into a cathedral close. Give it to the vicar, but don't fail to read it first.' – *Daily Express*

THE DOORS OPEN

An Inspector Hazlerigg mystery

One night on a commuter train, Paddy Yeatman-Carter sees a man about to commit suicide. Intervening, he prevents the man from going through with it. However, the very next day the same man is found dead, and Paddy believes the circumstances to be extremely suspicious. Roping in his friend and lawyer, Nap Rumbold, he determines to discover the truth. They become increasingly suspicious of the dead man's employer: the Stalagmite Insurance Company, which appears to hire some very dangerous staff.

'A well-written, cleverly constructed story which combines the unexpected with much suspicion and dirty work.'
– *Birmingham Mail*

Michael Gilbert

The Dust and the Heat

Oliver Nugent is a young Armoured Corps officer in the year 1945. Taking on a near derelict pharmaceutical firm, he determines to rebuild it and make it a success. He encounters ruthless opposition, and counteracts with some fairly unscrupulous methods of his own. It seems no one is above blackmail and all is deemed fair in big business battles. Then a threat: apparently from German sources it alludes to a time when Oliver was in charge of an SS camp, jeopardizing his company and all that he has worked for.

'Mr Gilbert is a first-rate storyteller.' – *The Guardian*

The Etruscan Net

Robert Broke runs a small gallery on the Via de Benci and is an authority on Etruscan terracotta. A man who keeps himself to himself, he is the last person to become mixed up in anything risky. But when two men arrive in Florence, Broke's world turns upside down as he becomes involved in a ring of spies, the Mafiosi, and fraud involving Etruscan antiques. When he finds himself in prison on a charge of manslaughter, the net appears to be tightening, and Broke must fight for his innocence and his life.

'Neat plotting, impeccable expertize and the usual shapeliness combine to make this one of Mr Gilbert's best.'
– *The Sunday Times*

MICHAEL GILBERT

FLASH POINT

Will Dylan is an electoral favourite – intelligent, sharp and good-looking, he is the government's new golden boy.

Jonas Killey is a small-time solicitor – single-minded, uncompromising and obsessed, he is hounding Dylan in the hope of bringing him into disrepute.

Believing he has information that can connect Dylan with an illegal procedure during a trade union merger, he starts to spread the word, provoking a top-level fluttering. At the crucial time of a general election, Jonas finds himself pursued by those who are determined to keep him quiet.

'Michael Gilbert tells a story almost better than anyone else.'
– *The Times Literary Supplement*

THE NIGHT OF THE TWELFTH

Two children have been murdered. When a third is discovered – the tortured body of ten-year-old Ted Lister – the Home Counties police are compelled to escalate their search for the killer, and Operation Huntsman is intensified.

Meanwhile, a new master arrives at Trenchard House School. Kenneth Manifold, a man with a penchant for discipline, keeps a close eye on the boys, particularly Jared Sacher, son of the Israeli ambassador...

'One of the best detective writers to appear
since the war.' – BBC

Made in the USA
Columbia, SC
18 March 2021